THE PARTING SHOT . . .

"Krantz!" Steele called softly into the shocked silence.

The broadly built man turned only his square face toward the Virginian. The stronger emotions were draining out of him, and his discolored teeth showed under his Mexican-style moustache in a grin of triumph and pride. "It was a fair fight, punk!" he rasped through the teeth.

"So is this, feller," Steele said.

The Colt Hartford was canted to his left shoulder. Krantz still had his matched Colts drawn. "You been askin' for it long enough, punk."

The hammers of the Colts and the Colt Hartford clickend back in perfect unison. But the rifle slammed down into the waiting palm faster than the revolvers were swung onto target. The naked terror of impending death showed in Krantz's eyes, revealing his knowledge that this was a fight he was doomed to lose.

The Colt Hartford cracked, and Krantz died with his eyes wide open, carrying into eternity the expression of fear.

"You want more money for killing your own?" Engle spat through lips set in the crooked line of a sneer.

"Not me, feller," the Virginian replied evenly as he ejected the spent shells from the rifle and fed fresh rounds into the cylinder's six chambers. He glanced down at the inert, loose-limbed, spread-eagled form of Krantz. "Never mix business with pleasure."

S0-AVS-333

THE ADAM STEELE SERIES:

WRITE FOR OUR FREE CATALOG

If there is a Pinnacle Book you want—and you cannot find it locally—it is available from us simply by sending the title and price plus 50¢ per order and 10¢ per copy to cover mailing and handling costs to:

Pinnacle Books, Inc.
Reader Service Department
2029 Century Park East
Los Angeles, California 90067

Please allow 4 weeks for delivery. New York State and California residents add applicable sales tax.

———Check here if you want to receive our catalog regularly.

No. 15

George G. Gilman

ADAM STEELE

RIVER OF DEATH

PINNACLE BOOKS • LOS ANGELES

This is a work of fiction. All the characters and
events portrayed in this book are fictional, and any
resemblance to real people or incidents is purely
coincidental.

STEELE #15: RIVER OF DEATH

Copyright © 1980 by George G. Gilman

All rights reserved, including the right to reproduce
this book or portions thereof in any form.

An original Pinnacle Books edition, published for
the first time anywhere.

First printing, January 1980

ISBN: 0-523-40525-1

Cover illustration by Fred Love

Printed in the United States of America

PINNACLE BOOKS, INC.
2029 Century Park East
Los Angeles, California 90067

for:
KEN AND SHIRLEY—
may Lady Luck be a friend
again soon.

RIVER OF DEATH

CHAPTER ONE

The midmorning sun was bright and blurred by heat haze. But there had been some heavy rain during the night somewhere in the north and the Mississippi was swollen: flowing fast towards New Orleans where it would begin its final run across the delta to the Gulf. The swift moving water was stained light brown by stirred up silt and its disturbed surface was liberally scattered with the driftwood of uprooted trees and brush.

From the northern fringe of a stand of timber three hundred feet east of the river bank, Adam Steele eyed the frantic rush of the Mississippi with mild distaste. The black mare beneath him vented a low snort of dissatisfaction, as if sensing and sharing the mood of its rider.

"Easy," Steele urged softly, stroking a gloved hand over the neck of the mare.

The animal calmed and dipped its head to crop at the lush turf which swept down to the river in a broad, gently sloping meadow. Steele allowed his gaze to rake northwards over the meadow, to study the ugliness of the settlement he knew to be Bradstock Landing.

It was not much of a place: just a half dozen crude shacks clustered around a jetty on the eastern shore of the river. On the opposite bank there was another jetty with just a single shack at its landward end. A ferry boat, large enough to carry a wagon and team, was being poled across the quarter mile wide river towards Bradstock Landing. Four ferrymen sweated at the back-breaking task. The single passenger remained mounted on his white horse, fanning himself with his hat. Smoke rising ramrod straight from the chimney of one of the shacks was the only other sign of human activity along this stretch of the river. The sternwheeler *Queen of the River* moored fore and aft to the marshy bank just north of the landing appeared to be as deserted—and derelict—as the shacks. For all that could be seen to move was the boat herself, riding with the flow of the river against the restraint of the mooring lines.

The mare snorted again, this time in resentment, when Steele demanded they move out of the shade of the timber to cross the meadow under the full glare of the Louisiana sun. He directed the horse to follow a line of trampled grass, the blades bent and broken by other riders who had recently crossed the meadow from trees to shacks.

Steele had not been out of the shadows for more than a few moments before he sensed interested eyes watching him. One of the watchers he could see—the mounted man aboard the ferry as the ponderous craft crossed the midway point of the fast flowing river. No wave of greeting was offered as the man continued to stir the hot air with his hat. Steele's gloved hands maintained their loose grip on the reins of the mare, and he shifted his gaze to the shacks with the boat just beyond. Still nobody could be seen in or around the landing, but Steele could feel scrutiny of his approach as strongly as he felt the rays of the sun on his back.

Like so much else which contributed to the man he had become, this component of a sixth sense had germinated during the blood-letting harshness of the War Between the States. The battles and the skirmishes, the

2

killing and the maiming, the destruction and wastefulness, the horrors and the terrors of the civil war were now many years in the past. And many men who had lived through the experience had chosen to forget the lessons they were forced to learn in order to survive. Some had chosen not to. A few had not been given the alternatives. Such a man was Adam Steele who had greeted the ending of the war with greater hope than most: only to have his hope dashed by the agonising outbreak of the violent peace. On the night Abraham Lincoln was shot, Steele's father was lynched from a beam in a Washington bar room.

Opposing loyalties to the Union and the Confederacy had caused a deep rift between father and son during the war. But after the peace signing at Appomattox the signs were good for a healing of the family wound. The son rode towards Washington in the sure and certain knowledge that he and his father would pick up the threads of what had once been and resume their rightful place as the most respected plantation owners in Virginia.

But he found Ben Steele senselessly dead—and committed his first murder without benefit of a lieutenant's uniform to make the act legal. Then he found the plantation house a burnt-out shell and the surrounding fields charred black by fire. He buried his father's remains on Steele land and rode towards the violent peace on the vengeance trail, carrying with him the hard-learned skills of war and a single material inheritance from his father—A Colt Hartford revolving rifle with an inscribed gold plate screwed to the fire-charred stock. The message on the plate read: *To Benjamin P. Steele, with gratitude—Abraham Lincoln.*

This rifle was in the boot now as Steele rode closer to the squalid shacks of Bradstock Landing. But the trampled grass beneath the hooves of the black mare was not

3

a part of that vengeance trail which had started at the burnt plantation in Virginia. That particular trail had ended long ago and it was fitting that the Colt Hartford had delivered the ultimate punishment to the group of fanatics who had murdered its first owner.

"You want somethin' in this place, mister?"

There were three shacks on either side of the east-west trail where it finished at the jetty, thus forming a kind of short street. Steele had rode on to this street and reined his mount to a halt when the question was growled at him. The man who spoke shuffled on to the threshold of a shack with the single word *Café* painted in crude lettering above the open doorway.

He was about sixty, completely bald but with a bushy moustache matching the grey color of his unshaven jaw. He was close to six feet tall and very thin. He wore a shirt with the sleeves cut off, denim pants and an apron stiff with ancient grease. His feet were bare. His eyes and mouthline were as unfriendly as his tone of voice.

Steele shook his head as he glanced around. "Somebody. Man named Cliff Engle."

The two shacks on the same side of the street as the café were simply houses. Directly opposite the café was a larger place with a painted sign proclaiming it was a hotel. Next to this was a general store. Then came the smallest building of the tiny community. This was adorned with a professionally painted sign, the weathered lettering naming it as *Landing Office*.

"Yeah?" the skinny six-footer countered with mild surprise. "You don't look like the others."

His expression showed a stronger emotion—something akin to contempt.

Steele eyed the man impassively. "You don't look like a man who runs the kind of place I'd choose to eat in, feller. Unless I was real hungry."

Steele's tone was as unrevealing as his face. The

skinny man elected to accept the response as an unmitigated insult: so he grimaced, spat forcefully at the hard-packed dirt of the street and withdrew into his café.

"You figure there's more to you than meets the eye, that right, stranger?"

The Virginian swung his head to look at the open doorway of the hotel. Three more men standing at close to six feet tall were crowded on the threshold. Two of them were grinning and a little excited. The third, who had spoken, looked bored. All were in their early thirties, with broad shoulders, narrow waists and the legs of men who spent a great deal of time in the saddle. Dressed predominantly in black they wore shirts, kerchiefs, vests, pants and spurred riding boots. The flesh of their faces and hands was sun bronzed and crinkled. Their holstered Colt revolvers looked well cared for and the bullets slotted into their gunbelts had a quality of newness as they glinted in the sunlight. Each had a glass fisted in a big hand, containing just the foam of old beer.

"If a man wants to put up money or an argument, he's entitled to find out," Steele answered.

The two grinning men became a little more excited as they switched their attention back and forth between Steele and their spokesman. The third of the trio was suddenly less bored as he became more concentrated in his study of the newcomer.

The man he was examining might have been a couple of years either side of thirty. He was not tall and, down from the horse, would stand perhaps a half inch more than five and a half feet. His build was slender but after more than a mere second glance it was obvious there was a compact strength at the command of the Virginian. The face was pleasant enough to look at, with even a kind of nondescript handsomeness in the regular features. It was a long face, stained brown by an outdoor

5

life and cut with lines by the passing years and the experiences of the past. The eyes were solid black, emphasized by the clear whiteness of their surrounds. The mouthline was gentle but something warned that was a trait of the man not to be entirely trusted. He was clean-shaven, but wore his sideburns long, composed of hair that was prematurely grey and showed just faint traces of the red it once had been.

His style of dress was more suitable for the paved streets and elegant buildings of New Orleans than the crude community of Bradstock Landing. For he wore a well-tailored city suit, grey with blue stitching at the lapels and cuffs of the jacket. Beneath the jacket was a purple vest and a white shirt with lace trim. His spurless riding boots, worn beneath the cuffs of his pants, were two-tone brown and white. His low-crowned grey Stetson was suitable for any surroundings.

Other items of clothing were at odds with the style and elegance of his general appearance: the scuffed and worn black buckskin gloves which fitted his hands tightly enough to contour every knuckle, the sweat-stained grey silk scarf which served as a kerchief, and the torn and patched sheepskin topcoat lashed to the bulky bedroll behind his saddle. These things were old and well used in contrast to the rest of his apparel which still showed store-bought newness under the dust of recent travel.

"I ain't never been one to invite trouble, stranger. Find it usually comes to a man without no invitation."

His companions stopped grinning to show disappointment laced with confusion.

"So we might as well have another damn beer," the one with a bullet scar across his jaw growled.

"Reckon so, Ned. Looks like today's gonna be the same as yesterday." He spoke with the same kind of Virginia drawl as Steele.

Both men swayed a little as they swung around to withdraw into the shade of the hotel.

"Engle ain't here yet," the lone man in the doorway announced. "Guy on the boat reckons he'll show up tonight."

Now he turned to go from sight inside the hotel. He was steadier on his feet than the other two.

"Grateful to you," Steele called after him, then swung down from the saddle.

The only hitching rail in the community was outside the Landing Office and he led the mare across to it.

"Hank'll pay you twenty dollars for the horse, mister. You want to sell the saddle and stuff, Hank'll have to see it first."

The woman was fat and unconcerned at the amount of bulbous flesh revealed by her open-to-the-waist bodice. She sat behind a rickety desk just inside the open doorway of the office, fanning herself with a sheaf of papers. The effort was self-defeating because the skin of her fleshy face and blue-veined chest and breasts remained sheened with tacky sweat. She was close to fifty and if she had ever been pretty there was no trace of it now. There was an avariciousness in her hard, flesh-squeezed eyes which hinted she was greedy for more than just food.

"I paid eighty for her three days ago, lady," Steele replied with disinterest as he slid the Colt Hartford out of the boot.

"Your problem, mister. Another problem you got is that Hank's the only feller around here interested in buyin' horses."

Steele nodded. "I have to talk to a man named Cliff Engle before I'll know if the horse is for sale."

The woman shrugged her shoulders and the dark brown nipples of her enormous breasts showed themselves in the vee of her open bodice for a moment. "No

7

rush, mister. When you're ready to do business, Hank ain't a hard man to find."

The Virginian canted the rifle to his right shoulder and angled across the street to the café. Nobody was watching him now. He had arrived at Bradstock Landing and been accepted. So interest had switched to the ferry which was docking at the jetty—primarily to the mounted passenger who was waiting patiently for the mooring lines to be secured and the side hatch to be lowered and form the gangplank.

Steele simply glanced at the man astride the white horse, noting he was out of the same Western mould as the men over at the hotel, then entered the café. The emaciated owner of the place backed away from him, irritated that he was to be denied a close up view of the second stranger to reach the landing.

"You're real hungry now, uh?" he growled, moving behind a counter that ran along the rear wall of the shack. The counter was formed by unplaned planks nailed to the tops of beer kegs. Behind it was an ancient range which had not been cleaned in a long time. Pots and pans and platters and cutlery were stacked on shelves to either side of the range. On the customers' side of the counter were three tables, each ringed by four chairs. The tables were as home made as the counter. The chairs were a mixture of wood and rattan, armed and armless, high-backed and backless. The place smelled of greasy cooking, tobacco smoke and sweat. Roaches scuttled out from under the feet of both men.

"Thirsty," Steele corrected, electing a high-backed, wooden armchair facing the window-flanked doorway of the café.

"Me and my brothers got an arrangement, mister. Hank runs the ferry, Pete operates the hotel and sells

8

liquor. I cook food. We don't horn in on each other's business."

"Where does a man get a cup of coffee?" Steele asked, watching the street through the open doorway.

"Oh, you want coffee. I figured that on a day like this you'd want . . ."

There was a fire in the range, sending up the only smoke which reached towards the heat hazed sky above the landing. The skinny man was suddenly happy that somebody other than himself wanted to make use of the reason for the fire. He poured coffee from the pot into a large tin mug and slopped a great deal on to the floor as he carried the order to the table.

"Sorry, mister." He tried a grin, but his toothless gums robbed his face of the expression he attempted. "About me being so unfriendly, like. But Hank and Pete been gettin' all the business this guy Engle's brought to the landing. That got me into a real mean mood. The coffee's good, mister. You try it and see. And don't you pay no attention to the kinda place I got. I cook food good as I brew up coffee. So if you get hungry, you just . . ."

"Gimme a coffee, feller. And some ham and beans. I guess you ain't got no eggs?"

It was the man who had crossed on the ferry. He barked his order in a harsh Texas drawl as he stepped into the café and folded his lanky frame into the chair nearest the door. This put his back to the room, but Steele had already seen he was about forty with a squarish, craggy face. His eyes were slits of light blue, his mouth was so narrow it seemed to have no lips and his nose was bent off-center from an old break that had never healed properly. He was in need of a shave and it had been a long time since he had last washed. There were white fringes on his blue shirt, his gunbelt and holster were tooled leather and his Remington revolver had a carved wooden grip.

"Comin' right up, sir," the skinny owner of the café responded enthusiastically. "Eggs I ain't got, but you'll get a meal to remember."

"Just need one that'll hold me until I eat next time." He glanced over his shoulder, ignoring the skinny man who had hurried back behind the counter: instead giving Steele a long, ice-cold look. "You here to do business with Engle?"

The Virginian was sipping his coffee, holding the mug in both gloved hands with his elbows leaning on the rifle which was rested on the two arms of his chair.

"Maybe, feller."

"You don't carry a handgun that I can see." He could see nothing of Steele now, for his coffee had been delivered and he had turned his head again: to peer out at the sunlit street as he sipped the strong, black, hot liqiud. "Just a Colt Hartford sporting rifle. You have to be good with that, or you'd have a Winchester these days."

"You with Engle, feller?" Steele asked evenly.

"Right now I'm with me. If the price is right, I'll be with Engle. Which could mean we'll be working together. So how you handle yourself in a tight corner is my business."

Fat sizzled in a skillet on the range. Fresh cooking smells began to mask the bad odors clinging to the café and its owner. The coffee was as good as the skinny man had promised and, as the ham began to fry, an even more appetising aroma permeated the fetid atmosphere.

"Why is that, feller?" the Virginian asked. "You can't take care of yourself?"

The Texan became suddenly rigid on the chair. And a vein at the side of his neck bulged a blue ridge against the sun burnished flesh. Steele tensed himself to release the almost empty coffee mug and snatch at the rifle. But then the Texan laughed. The stiffness drained out of him and he turned his head slowly, showing that his thin lips were split to display rows of even teeth. And there was easy warmth in the blueness of his narrow eyes.

The skinny cook's sigh of relief was loud enough to be heard against the sizzle of the frying ham.

"That's good enough for me, dude," the Texan assured. "Figure you ain't the kind to call a man like me 'less you felt you could win. Name's Conners. Marv Conners. From Texas."

"Adam Steele," the Virginia responded with an easy grin of his own—an expression that cancelled out his prematurely grey hair and made him look much younger—even boyish. "From all over. New Orleans last stop." He stood up and glanced towards the skinny cook. "How much, feller?"

"Two cents."

Steele dropped a nickel on the table beside his empty mug, canted the rifle to his shoulder and went towards the door. "It's worth more. But I'll be back later for the other three cents' worth."

"Watch them three over at the hotel, Steele," Conners warned as the Virginian went around his table. "Breen's a good enough man on his own. But Fargo and McCall might stir him into something."

Steele acknowledged the warning with a short nod and stepped out on to the street. The air, tangy with the scent of the river, smelled good after breathing the confined atmosphere of the café. The Mississippi made gurgling sounds and there was a hum of talk punctuated by gusts of laughter from the hotel. Otherwise, a soporific silence was clamped down over Bradstock Landing.

11

Conners's white gelding was hitched to the rail beside Steele's mare outside the Landing Office.

"You got good gear, mister. Give you forty bucks for the horse and all that's on her. 'Cepting for the bedroll, course."

Hank was younger than his brother who ran the café. But only by two or three years. There was a family resemblance in the features of the two men, but their builds were totally different. Hank was broad and solid, his muscles well developed from poling the ferry back and forth across the river. His torso bulged his shirt now, as he leaned against the jamb of the office doorway.

"Same as I told the lady, feller," Steele responded, moving on beyond the office to the bank of the river.

"That ain't no lady, that's my wife!" Hank called, and roared with confident laughter.

"Smart mouth!" the fat woman shrieked.

Steele moved along the band, away from the jetty and towards the *Queen of the River*. Nothing about her backed up the regality implicit in her name. Perhaps once there had been, but she was old and had been illused. She was about a hundred feet from stem to stern and some thirty feet across the beam. Two decks high with a wheelhouse amidships. Her hull was painted black and her superstructure white. The paint was peeling in many places and stained dark brown with rust runs from neglected metal fittings. Her smokestacks had been patch-repaired many times. But her boiler and eighteen foot stern-wheel looked in good condition to the untrained eye of the Virginian.

"You seem enough, little man!"

"Whether you have or you ain't, best you back off! Not unless you got tired of totin' that head around on your shoulders!"

The two men were up in the wheelhouse. Steele had

seen them while he was making his survey of the stern-wheeler, watching him closely as he strolled to a point on the bank level with the paddlewheel. A window in the wheelhouse was flung wide and the growling words were hurled down at him as he made the return trip towards the bows. The men were naked to the waist, their flesh sheened with sweat and streaked with dirt from working. The taller of the two thrust a double barrelled shotgun out of the window as he delivered his threat.

The Virginian touched the brim of his hat. "It's got me into more trouble than enough, fellers. But I'm kind of attached to it."

The man without a gun, who was about twenty, blond-haired and almost girlishly handsome, greeted Steele's response with a gust of belly laughter.

"Friggin' wise guy!" the other one snarled. "Beat it! And if you're here to see the owner, wait at the landing until tonight!"

As Steele neared the huddle of buildings, Fargo and McCall emerged from the street and onto the jetty. One was dragging two chairs behind him and the other carried a bottle of whiskey. The chairs were set on the planking and the men sat down, faces to the sun and backs towards the approaching Virginian. The bottle was passed between the men, each up-ending it to his mouth.

"You get the shotgun waved at you?" the bullet-scarred Ned muttered as Steele drew close.

"To set you runnin' off like a spooked jackrabbit," the one with greasy black hair down to his shoulders augmented. "Without puttin' up no argument."

Steele halted in a casual stance and pursed his lips to vent a low sigh. He had come to Bradstock Landing expecting to find trouble, for the way in which he had been offered a job working for a man named Cliff Eagle

13

had made it obvious his potential employer was in a troublesome business. Therefore he had pulled on the buckskin gloves as he neared the end of the two day ride from New Orleans to the landing. Gloves that were a relic of the war: a paradox in that he, a man who set little store by luck, regarded them as some kind of charm—to be donned whenever and wherever violence threatened to explode.

He had not expected trouble so soon, though. And he was not prepared to welcome it until somebody was paying him to handle it. But neither was he surprised by the attitude of the two liquored-up gunmen who were spoiling for a fight. For he was familiar with the difficulties and disadvantages of appearing to be a square peg in a round hole. Ever since that day, long ago, when he had murdered his best friend and had forever cut all ties with the kind of life he had intended to live, men like Fargo and McCall—and Breen and Conners—had been thick on the ground. Frontier guns for hire who looked the part. Most of them experts or at least capable when they had a job to do. Some, and the two men sunning themselves on the jetty were of this kind, had such a keen appetite for trouble that they could not live without it. So when none came to them, they had to create it.

And a man like Adam Steele was a prime target: a dude with a gun as fancy as his clothes. Soft spoken and easy smiling. Cast from an entirely different mould than the likes of Fargo and McCall, for some reason he inspired resentment by his tacit claim to be one of their kind.

Both men snapped their heads around as Steele took a step onto the jetty, making no attempt to set down his boot lightly. Surprise was inscribed across their unshaven faces for a moment and it was obvious they had expected the Virginian to ignore their taunts and pass

14

on by. But his expressionless face and the way he continued to keep the Colt Hartford canted to his shoulder gave them back their liquor-edged confidence.

"I got as much as I needed," the Virginian said, moving closer to the men. "What is it you two fellers reckon you need?"

He shot a fast glance up along the street and saw that he had two spectators in the open. Marv Conners at the doorway of the café, holding a mug of coffee; and Breen in front of the hotel, drinking from a beer glass. Two more guns for hire who looked the part, but with the intelligence or experience to read what lay behind the nonchalant attitude of the Virginian.

"Not you around when the crap starts to fly, that's for sure!" Ned snarled.

"Damn right! Back off and ride outta town, you fancied up dandy!"

Steele showed no facial response to the hurled abuse; he merely came to an easy halt four feet from where the two men sat. "Guess that is what's called straight talking," he replied evenly. "Can you shoot just as straight with all that whiskey inside you?"

Ned spread a broad grin across his face and transferred the bottle to his left hand before he eased upright and turned slowly to face Steele across the back of the chair. "Hey, Fargo, this pretty-dressed guy is callin' us, ain't he?"

"McCall!" Breen yelled from in front of the hotel. "I warned you about him!"

Steele heard the crash of a dropped glass and then a heavy footfall on the hard-packed street. But he did not make the mistake of taking his eyes off the already standing Ned McCall and the rising Fargo.

"Hold it right there, Will!" Conners barked. "About time them two dumb clucks fought their own battle, wouldn't you say?"

The Virginian heard a grunt of anger from Breen as the man froze after the first stride of a run. Then the clicks of metal on metal as the Texan cocked his fast-drawn Remington.

The action on the street unsettled Fargo and McCall. Either they had fully expected help from Breen, or had finally spotted that in the Virginian's case appearance could be deceptive. Steele, outwardly calm—and sweating no more than the late morning heat merited—pushed the two men from fear into panic by simply using a thumb to click back the Colt Hartford's hammer.

Fargo snatched a glance towards McCall, looking for a signal.

McCall drew. He was fast, but a brain dulled by alcohol and assaulted by fear made his action clumsy.

The Colt Hartford whipped down from its slope. Steele's free hand came up from his side across his body, palm cupped to accept and then clasp the barrel.

Several people—men and women—shouted from their vantage points at doors and windows. The rifle shot cracked across the voices and silenced them. McCall's revolver was at half cock when the bullet slammed into the cylinder and wrenched the gun from the big hand. It turned end over end, hit the jetty with two bounces and plopped into the muddy water below.

"Sonofabitch!" McCall yelled, shaking his hand frantically to ease the pain in his fingers.

Fargo had his Colt half out of the holster when Steele made a quarter turn, cocking the rifle's action again and drawing a bead on the bigger man's gun hand.

"Don't!" Breen screamed.

Fargo took just part of a second to decide the demand was made of him. He uncurled his fingers from around the Colt's butt and stretched his arms stiffly into the air, hands clawed as if he was trying to grip solid in the hazy, humid air. He stared at Steele with watery

16

eyes and his mouth gaped wide, lips trembling. Ned McCall's face expressed a mixture of pain and hatred as he pressed his bruised hand into the opposite armpit.

His blazing eyes seemed to emanate a physical pressure against Steele's face as the Virginian closed in on Fargo, lifted the man's Colt from its holster and tossed it down into the Mississippi.

"We can get new ones at the store, smart guy!" McCall snarled. "Get your stupid hands down, Duke!"

"Is it all right to do like he says?" Fargo asked nervously as Steele canted the rifle to his shoulder.

"Do anything you like, feller. But keep in mind that the store doesn't sell new lives."

"Sure, sure!" Fargo blubbered.

"Shuddup, Duke!" McCall rasped, after taking another swig from the bottle he still grasped firmly in his uninjured hand. "This prettied up guy got off a lucky shot is all. Don't mean we have to toady to him."

Steele was passing in front of the scar-faced man whose dark green eyes now expressed only fuming hatred. Which was abruptly replaced by angry shock as the much smaller Virginian lunged sideways at him, to crash a shoulder into the broad chest. Taken completely by suprise, McCall was sent into an ungainly backward stagger flailing arms about him to try to regain his balance. He almost succeeded, but by then only the toes of his boots were on the edge of the jetty. He teetered there for a moment: then, with an animalistic roar of rage, toppled backwards to crash into the mud-colored water of the Mississippi.

"Cool off, feller," Steele muttered as McCall splashed with his arms and kicked with his legs to stand upright in the waist-deep shallows at the angle of bank and jetty.

"Why, if I get . . ."

"Do like the man told you, Ned!" Breen snapped,

released from the threat of Conner's Remington and stepping on to the jetty. "And remember you owe him twice over."

"Owe that sonofabitch?" McCall roared, shaking his head and scattering droplets of water from his face and hair. "Why I . . ."

"Yeah. He could've blasted the stupid life out of you. Or tossed you in where the river's deep."

"He'll be real sorry he didn't!" the soaking man snarled, and started to claw his way up the muddy bank. "Next time . . ."

"Could be I'll drown my sorrow," Steele cut in evenly with a quiet smile. "Come hell or high water."

CHAPTER TWO

More men with hard eyes, unshaven faces, travel-stained clothes and horses, and guns in tied-down holsters drifted into Bradstock Landing during hot afternoon. Two riding as a pair came in from the west, needing the services of Hank and his three muscular sons to pole them across the Mississippi on the ferry. Three others arrived at different times on the short cut route from New Orleans which Steele had used. Two more, recently strangers to each other but travelling together, reached the landing on the east trail.

"Stan and Andy Clapham," Conners told Steele of the brothers who crossed on the ferry. "Only thing they do better than killin' is herd cows."

He and the Virginian were in the café, sharing the table by the door and a pot of coffee which the skinny cook replaced as soon as it was empty.

"Grateful to you for holding off Breen," Steele had said when he re-entered the café after the trouble on the jetty.

"So's Breen," Conners had responded, waving Steele into the chair across the table from him and calling for the first pot of coffee. "Though he'd never say so. Same as he'd never thank you for not blastin' holes in those crazy sidekicks of his."

"What's between them, feller?"

A shrug of the broad shoulders. "Just know they've

19

been a team for a lot of years. Work real fine together by all accounts. But when there's no work Fargo and McCall—especially that dumbster McCall—always get to drinkin' and stirrin' the crap. But ain't neither of them any artist in a showdown, so Will Breen always has to finish their fights for them."

"Breen's good?"

"Best there is around Texas. Only trouble is, he fights fair. Beats me and a lot of other people how he's managed to stay alive so long."

They ate lunch together and Steele discovered that the skinny owner of the café had not lied about his prowess as a cook. The food was plain and plentiful, which was expected of a café in a place like Bradstock Landing. But it was also well cooked.

The Texan and the Virginian did not talk for a long time. Hank and his fat wife—the bodice of her dress buttoned to a more modest level—came to eat in the café. They were joined by the three handsome boys who helped run the ferry, one of these with a dusky-skinned wife. There was a constant flow of low-voiced conversation from the family group. But the brother who ran the hotel and his wife who worked the general store ate in stony silence.

Breen, McCall and Fargo remained over at the hotel where they had been since their return from the jetty—making a short stop at the store for the angry McCall and chastened Fargo to purchase new handguns.

For a while, Steele and Conners rested low in their chairs, hats tipped forward to hold the sunlight out of their eyes. It wasn't until a shout from across the river sent Hank and his sons hurrying to work that the Texan stirred, rising to go to the door and peer out at the new arrivals. Then he returned to the table to tell Steele who they were.

"You know a lot of people, feller."

Conners shook his head. "I know somethin' about a lot of people, Steele. People in my line of work. Out of professional interest, you might say. Just stuff I pick up goin' along. It don't do to pry, does it? Of men in our line of work?"

The Virginian straightened in his chair and set his hat back on top of his head. And saw the question behind the warmth of a smile in the slitted blue eyes of the man opposite him.

Steele showed a smile of his own and accompanied it with a short nod. "My line of work happens to be whatever's available when I need a job, feller."

"That wasn't no lucky shot that took the gun clean outta McCall's hand. But you'd have been quite willin' to waste him and Fargo both, if that was the way the breaks fell."

There was an air of caution about the way Conners spoke and looked. Steele had already proved his easygoing attitude was not to be trusted and Conners had acknowledged that asking the wrong questions of the wrong man could be dangerous.

"I shot fine before the war, feller," Steele allowed without resentment. "In the war it came in useful for killing fine. Since then I've always done what I had to."

"Knife, too?"

Conners leaned to the side of the table and glanced briefly at the outside of Steele's right pants leg. When he straightened, his eyebrows were arched. He added: "And that kerchief ain't just a kerchief, is it?"

The knife, kept in a boot sheath and accessible through a split in the seam of his pants, was like the buckskin gloves. He had taken to carrying such a weapon in such a manner when he was a Confederate cavalry lieutenant.

The silk scarf had been acquired during the ven-

21

geance hunt for his father's killers. With a lead weight sewn into two diagonally opposite corners, it was of Oriental origin—a thuggee weapon of strangulation.

"Horses for courses," Steele responded cryptically.

Conners shrugged again. "Sure, Steele." He poured another mug of coffee for himself and topped up the Virginian's mug. "Only weapon I'm any good with is this old Remington." A broad grin. "And my fists if I figure a man don't deserve to get dead all the way. You've proved yourself and I ain't got no right nor no reason to ask no questions. I'm just one hell of a curious guy is all."

"You can say that again," Steele countered softly as the Clapham brothers halted outside, undecided whether to kill time in the café or the hotel.

"Marv," one of the black-bearded, bulbous-bellied men of forty-some greeted.

The other simply nodded.

"Stan. Andy." Conners raised a hand in a lazy greeting. "Will Breen and his two sidekicks are over to the hotel."

"Been a long time," Stan said. "See you later, uh?"

"Be good to work with you again," Conners acknowledged.

The brothers ambled across and into the hotel, neither having given Steel more than a perfunctory glance.

"Like old home week," the Virginian muttered.

Conners grinned some more. "All of us are Texas boys. Born there or been there a long time. But you got nothin' to worry about. Stan and Andy'll hear about you from Will Breen and it'll be enough for them."

Steele felt a stir of hot anger at the pit of his stomach. But he had long ago learned to conceal his emotions—and to control his innate temper by realising it could get him killed. So his face was impassive and his tone even

22

when he said: "I heard it was a feller named Engle who was offering me a job."

Conners was intelligent enough to know he had scraped a raw nerve. "Ain't I the clumsy one? Forget it, Steele. It's just that we Texans figure we're somethin' special. Like . . . aw hell, you been around enough to find out the kind of breed we are, ain't you?"

"I reckon," the Virginian answered with an easy smile. "Big men with big hearts from a big state. Everything big. Including your feet and the mouths you put them in."

Conners tensed into rigidity, just as he had done shortly after he first entered the café. Now, as then, he abruptly relaxed with a gust of laughter. "Damn right, Steele! And I reckon there's lots of people who'd tell you I'm the champ at doin' that!"

Another comfortable silence settled between them as the afternoon progressed, the heat staying high and humid. The owner of the place fell asleep, his bony rump propped on a stool and his upper body sprawled across the counter top. He snored discreetly, the regular beat of his breathing counterpointing the sounds of the flowing river.

Later, Conners nodded into sleep. Steele went outside and discovered the Clapham brothers had hitched their geldings to the rail outside the landing office. Although the doors of all the buildings were open, there was no sight or sound of anybody, until his ears separated from the noises of the river the easy breathing and harsh wheezing of other people who slept.

Doing no favour to anyone, but concerned for the welfare of the horses, he unhitched all four animals and took them down to the river bank to drink. Then he led them out back of the landing office and hitched them to the rear wheel of a buckboard, in the shade and on a

23

patch of grass. It was while he was attending to this chore that a youngster of about twenty came across the meadow, riding slow with his head constantly on the move as he surveyed the terrain on all sides. His attire was city-style, complete with derby hat, but the clothes were cheaper and a lot less fancy than Steele's. He wore his gunbelt under his jacket, but with one side of the suit top pulled back to leave the butt of the Colt exposed at the top of the holster.

He was thin and tall, his clothing seeming to hang on his frame rather than to fit it. His face had a pale, city complexion with hollow cheeks, a prominent nose and a jutting jaw line. There was a kind of arrogant bravado in his grey eyes as he took off his hat, ran a long fingered hand through his slicked down black hair, and asked: "Where do I find Clifford Engle?"

His accent said that he was completely at home in the deep south; his tone suggested he felt he was superior to the man he was addressing.

"That's the fifty dollar question, kid," Steele replied. "If you've been offered the same daily rate as me."

The youngster blinked, perturbed by the response. But he recovered his disdainful composure very quickly. "You mean he's not here?"

"Rumour has it he'll be by tonight, kid. Gives you plenty of time to impress the Texans."

"I beg your pardon?" He blinked his eyes several times now.

"At fifty dollars a day you don't need to beg."

He left the quartet of horses to crop at the shaded grass and went along the side of the landing office. Behind him the youngster dismounted and hitched his own animal to the buckboard. Steele was back at the café table when the newcomer emerged on to the short street. Like an animal, Marv Conners did not jerk out of sleep until he heard the unfamiliar footfalls of the

24

youngster crossing towards the café. He simply raised and pushed back his head to peer out from under the brim of his tipped forward hat.

"Don't know him," he drawled. "Young punk out to make a rep for himself, looks like."

"You when you were his age?" Steele suggested.

"Nah. I got started late."

When the newcomer stepped into the café Conners had allowed his chin to drop forward on to his chest, apparently fast asleep again.

"They call me City Sam Goldsmith," the kid growled, dropping into a chair at the next table. Then he raised his voice. "Hey, how about some coffee for a thirsty man, skinny!"

The owner of the place came awake with a start.

"That's too long, boy," Conners muttered from under his hat. "Guess I'll just call you plain Loudmouth."

"Sure, coffee comin' up, sir," the man behind the counter said fast, almost toppling over his stool as he hurried to the range.

Goldsmith was not shocked by the soft-spoken insult. Merely angry. It showed in his face, the way the skin stretched taut across his prominent bone structure. His movements were slow as he placed both hands carefully on the table top. "You want to step outside and repeat that, Tex?" he asked.

"Why, boy? You got somethin' against dying under a roof?" Conners, too, was slow spoken and lazy moving as he came upright on his chair and tipped his Stetson on to the back of his head.

"Please, I don't want no trouble in my place," the skinny owner of the café implored, hurrying to bring a mug of steaming coffee to Goldsmith's table. "And none of us want any trouble at the landin' at all."

Conners made the mistake of looking away from the boy to the man, his lips forming the first word of a re-

25

sponse. And Goldsmith saw the opportunity. His right hand was snatched from the table top, fingers curling to fist around the butt of the Colt.

The Texan vented a grunt of self-anger and only had a fingertip touch on his holstered Remington when the Colt was clear of the table, levelled and cocked.

The skinny cook uttered a groan of desperation and took a backward step.

Steele pushed out his rifle to the side, stock first. Then angled it sharply upwards. The stock cracked into the bottom of the mug and scalding hot coffee was sprayed out of the top.

Goldsmith shrieked, pain contorting his features into emaciated ugliness as the steaming black liquid doused his jaw and neck. Instinctively, he pushed himself backwards with his feet and brought up both hands to the source of his agony. His chair tipped and fell and he was spilled out of it.

The Texan had his Remington aimed then, standing up and tracking the course of the groaning youngster.

"I don't reckon he deserves to get dead all the way, feller," Steele said. "All he did was to get a little hot under the collar."

"You bastards!" Goldsmith snarled, hauling himself into a sitting position with his back against the door frame. He still held the Colt, but kept it down between his knees under the threat of the aimed Remington. "It took two of you to get the drop on me."

"Which maybe proves you're real good at what you want to be, kid," the Virginian suggested. "I'm impressed and I reckon Conners is?"

He shot a sidelong glance at the Texan and saw that the man was trying to conceal something akin to humiliation behind a brittle veneer of rage.

"I oughta make an impression on the ass of the little snotnose!" the Texan snarled between clenched teeth.

26

He continued to counter Goldsmith's stare of hatred with one of his own. Then he uncocked the Remington and twirled it by the trigger-guard before sliding it back into his holster.

He sat down and glared at the nervous cook. "Pot of coffee, uh? The boy'll join us."

The youngster got to his feet and the sneer on his thin face hinted he was about to vent another insult as he pushed his Colt into the holster.

"Glad to be of service to you gentlemen," the cook blurted, whirling to scuttle over to the range.

"The fight's over, kid," Steele said evenly. "Don't make it into a war."

Conners nodded his agreement.

"Okay," Goldsmith allowed, pulling back his shoulders and dusting off his suit with his hands before taking a chair at the table. "But you men just remember what my name is."

"He's Conners," the Virginian answered. "I'm Steele."

They drank coffee together and the youngster smoked strong-smelling cheroots. He offered the others a smoke before he lit his third one and was turned down with shaking heads. There was no further talk until other men began coming to Bradstock Landing.

"Don't know 'em," Conners growled of the two who rode in on the east trail.

"The one with no left ear is Frank Potter," Goldsmith offered. "One time gambler on the Missouri riverboats. Now he keeps trouble away from the house of ill repute in New Orleans where his wife is the madam. The man with him is a stranger to me."

The gambler turned bordello minder was in his early fifties with the same kind of pale, city complexion as the boy. He was tall and broad but a great deal of his bulk was flab. He was dressed Western style with the

27

exception of the riverman's peak cap: all the clothing was brand new. There was a certain unctuous charm in the set of his smooth-skinned, regular features. The lack of a left ear gave his head an odd, lop-sided look.

After both men had used the landing office hitching rail to hold their horses, Potter entered the hotel. His younger travelling companion came into the café. There had been no talk between the newcomers.

"Afternoon all. You people for the *Queen of the River* picnic?"

He was in his late twenties, of medium height, build and good looks. His skin was sun burnished but carried few lines. He had an easy smile and a loose-limbed way of moving. He took off his Stetson as he entered the café to show short cut, neatly trimmed black hair. He wore a black suit, white shirt and black bootlace tie. Even though his jacket was unbuttoned, its drape was spoiled by the bulge of a gun he carried in a left shoulder holster.

"Engle won't be here until tonight," Steele supplied after a nod to acknowledge the man's greeting.

"Name's Clint Burton. From Boston by way of New York, Chicago, San Francisco and New Orleans. A great many lesser places in between."

He supplied this information in response to the tacit inquiries from the hard eyes of Conners and Goldsmith.

"You've been a lot of places," the boy said with a trace of a smile. He used a boot to push the fourth chair away from the table and it was obvious he was prepared to accept Burton at face value. Perhaps on a hunch, or maybe because he felt they were equals. Certainly, Burton's well modulated New England accent suggested he had enjoyed as fine an education as Goldsmith.

"Another mug," Conners called, the words allowing Burton into the group but the tone in which he spoke them indicating that he held reservations.

"Real kind of you."

After he had poured himself a coffee Burton began to talk about himself and the cities he had visited. But when he failed to draw any enthusiastic responses from the others he seemed content to share their silence.

"Vic Krantz," Goldsmith announced just as afternoon was darkening towards evening and another gunman rode into Bradstock Landing across the meadow from the timber. "Reckoned to be the meanest plantation foreman in the whole of Louisiana and Mississippi. That bullwhip isn't just for show."

After hitching his horse, Krantz paused just a moment before going into the hotel—to look through the café doorway and glower malevolently.

"That meant for you, City Sam?" Burton asked.

The youngster grinned and ran a hand through his black hair in a gesture of pure arrogance. "There was a girl and some trouble. Krantz won't ever forget about it—until the day I kill him."

Conners vented a low grunt of scorn, still smarting from being beaten to the draw by the youngster.

Krantz was about forty, matching the height of Steele but a lot broader with muscular development. His head seemed to rest between his shoulders with no neck in between. He had a ruddy-skinned face cast in squarish lines and the curves of his Mexican-style moustache looked out of place. He wore a two-holster gunbelt atop the check shirt draped outside his denim pants, and carried a coiled bullwhip. He limped slightly, favouring his right leg.

The sun was red, staining the western sky and the river the same color when the third man rode in off the meadow. He was in his late twenties, dressed entirely in black—hat, shirt, vest, pants and boots. He did not wear a gunbelt but after he had dismounted at the jetty, he drew a Winchester rifle from the boot. After he had hobbled the forelegs of his black gelding he squatted on his haunches and became like a statue of carved black stone as he peered out at the river.

"Don't know him," Conners growled.

"Nor me," Goldsmith added.

"I'm not a social animal," Steele contributed.

Nobody looked at Burton until he said, in his cultured accent: "Ricardo Sanchez. A professional bodyguard. He was working for one of the Central Pacific railroad barons in San Francisco the last time I saw him."

"Before that?" Conners asked, deeply interested in adding to his store of information about fellow gunslingers.

"One other time," the Bostonian answered, accepting a cheroot and a light from Goldsmith. "Staked out up in the Uinta Mountains east of Salt Lake City. With his tongue cut out and his testicles pulped."

"A quiet killer, uh?" Conners said with a grin.

"He doesn't like jokes about being dumb, Mr. Conners," Burton warned. "And it's best if you treat ladies with respect when the Mexican is around. It seems that since he was emasculated he has become extremely protective towards females."

As if she had been waiting for a cue, a woman over at the hotel vented a high pitched scream. The sun was completely set now and the gathering gloom of dusk seemed to intensify the instant of silence which followed the abruptly curtailed cry.

"Pete's wife," the skinny man behind the counter gasped.

"Come 'ere, you stupid cow!" a man bellowed.

Footfalls beat at a floor inside the hotel. Then the homely, full-bodied, middle-aged wife of the hotel owner burst out through the doorway, her hands pressed to her breasts to hold the torn bodice of her dress together. Other, heavier footfalls hit the floor. The woman skidded to a halt in the center of the street and snapped her head to left and right in search of escape. Stark terror was inscribed on her puffy, blotchy face. She was about to run towards the river, but something in that direction scared her. Of the group of men who came out of the café, only her brother-in-law was familiar.

"Rob!" she shrieked, big eyes imploring help.

The one-eared Frank Potter charged out of the hotel doorway, his usually wan face glowing red with excitement. He slowed suddenly when he saw the woman had halted, and closed in on her at a measured walk. The grin of triumph pasted to his features made him look grotesquely ugly.

Behind him, the doorway spilled Breen and McCall and Fargo, Stan and Andy Clapham, Vic Krantz, and Pete. With the exception of the hapless husband of the terrified woman—who seemed as frightened as she was—the men regarded the scene on the street with mild interest.

Until the first rifle shot cracked through the warm, twilight air. Then, in common with Conners, Goldsmith and Burton the men across the street reached for their guns. None left its holster, though. For eyes had had time to flick towards the black-clad figure of Sanchez and back towards where the bullet had kicked up dirt in front of Potter's boots. A second shot followed the first with only the scraping of the Winchester's lever action separating them. The bullet struck the ground a fraction of an inch away from Potter's heels.

The Mexican was firing from the shoulder as he strode up from the jetty: riding with the recoil and not allowing the barrel to waver as he pumped the action. A third shot sprayed dirt up the side of Potter's pants leg.

31

The skinny Rob pushed between Conners and Steele and ran onto the street. The woman staggered towards his outstretched arms.

Potter recovered from long moments of frozen terror. His feet remained firmly planted to the ground, but he bent his legs as he turned to face the advancing Mexican—and streaked a hand to his holstered Tranter.

"He could hit your heart at four times the range!" Clint Burton yelled.

Sanchez had come to a halt the moment the woman was embraced by her brother-in-law. His aim was rock steady, the muzzle of the Winchester no longer angled down towards the ground.

Beads of sweat squeezed out of the pores on Potter's face, and formed rivulets down over the skin which was now pale again. He remained in the half-turned, half-crouched attitude, right-hand fisted around the butt of the still-holstered gun.

"Ain't he sure enough of that to speak up for himself?" the one-eared man snarled, hoarse-voiced.

"He can't speak about anything," Burton explained, even-voiced as Pete left the hotel doorway and scuttled in a wide half-circle to reach his weeping wife. "Indian trouble."

"Sure can shoot, though," Ned McCall rasped.

Sanchez made a fast gesture with his right hand: miming the act of drawing a gun from a holster and tossing it away.

"Like hell I will!" Potter snarled.

"What's the difference, bud?" the bearded, pot-bellied Stan Clapham pointed out lazily. "If he wanted to plug you, he could do it. Gun or no."

Pete was trying to pry his wife out of the arms of his brother. The woman interrupted her sobs for long enough to hiss an obscenity at him. Then she hit him back-handed across the face. Nobody paid any attention to this side action to the main attraction.

Suddenly, the Mexican bobbed down into a crouch, raised the muzzle of the rifle and squeezed off a shot. The bullet snagged at the underside of Potter's riverman's cap and sent the headgear high into the air.

Surprise slowed Potter's reflexes. And by the time he started to draw his Tranter the rifleman was erect again, the action of the Winchester pumped and the muzzle trained on the heart of the one-eared man. The barrel of the revolver was only half out of the holster.

"Frig it, bud, you're beat all ends up," Andy Clapham snapped, and broke from the group in the hotel doorway.

He closed in on the back of Potter, grasped the half drawn Tranter around the cylinder and jerked it out of its owner's hand. He stared at the gun with blatant scorn for a moment, then turned and ambled back to rejoin the group.

Sanchez started towards Potter.

"Kill him and you'll be another hunk of fish food," Stan Clapham warned, jerking a thumb towards the river.

Potter held still, except for a nervous twitch of the fingers of his empty gunhand.

"He didn't hurt me, mister!" the woman blurted out, tearing away from Rob's embrace. "It's just he had too much to drink and . . ."

She curtailed her plea, aware from the relentless advance of the Mexican that he was not listening.

It was probable that he also failed to hear or see the approaching wagon train rumbling slowly towards Bradstock Landing on the east trail. Potter likewise. Everyone else glanced out along the trail for long enough to count six covered wagons drawn by ox teams, then returned their attention to the street.

Sanchez came to an almost military halt immediately in front of the sweating Potter. He had Latin good looks, with dark eyes, a fine bone structure and dusky skin. His expression was entirely devoid of emotion. But his eyes at close quarters aroused more fear in Potter than the rifle muzzle aimed at his heart.

"What's she to you, mister?" the one-eared man groaned. "Hell, if anyone oughta be roustin' me, should be her old man. Why, I was only havin' a little fun with her. Like she said, I drank more than . . ."

The Mexican's only facial response to the blubbering excuse was to form his thin lips into a contemptuous sneer. Then he exploded into movement. First a half turn, to fling the Winchester away from him. Not carelessly, though. The direction and power of the throw was finely judged—so that Clint Burton merely had to take one step forward to catch the rifle in a two handed grip. Then an equally well aimed knee was thudded into Potter's crotch.

The heavier man vented his shock and pain with a low-keyed moan and staggered backwards as he folded from the waist. Sanchez went after him, reaching out both hands to grip the hair at each side of Potter's head. The same knee which had delivered the initial blow was sent into the face of the moaning man. Potter uttered a strangled groan and the Mexican's pants were stained darkly with blood from the burst vessels of his victim's nose.

Potter had tried to fend off the second attack, bringing up his hands from the agony at his crotch. But he was too late. Then too weakened to do anything but drop to his rump when the Mexican released him, he sat there, arms loosely at his sides, head raised to display his bloodied nose and his eyes which pleaded for the punishment to be over.

But Sanchez moved forward, placing a foot either

34

side of Potter's knees, and dropped to his haunches. Then he began to hit Potter—his palm slapping one cheek and the back of the same hand attacking the other. Potter's head snapped back and forth, spraying droplets of blood in each direction. Two, four, six, eight . . . the paired blows continued to crack into flesh. Too weak to retaliate, Potter's sole part of the beating was simply to suffer it for as long as he could: drawing what comfort he could from exhibiting his ability to endure.

And he was still sitting upright, with his entire face run with blood, when the man driving the first wagon reined his ox team to a halt on the street. And a grimly angry man who had been riding on the passenger seat leapt to the ground to roar:.

"I'm Clifford J. Engle! Just what in tarnation is goin' on here?"

The man who everyone was waiting to see received a series of glances, then was ignored by all except Adam Steele.

"That feller is beating up that other feller," the Virginian replied against the regular crack of a hand on a face in an exhibition of brutality and suffering which held a hard-eyed audience virtually spellbound.

The city-suited, immaculately groomed Engle glowered at Steele then addressed himself to everyone on the street again: "Listen to me, you men! If you want to work for me, you'll stop this immediately!"

Sanchez halted the beating and eased to his feet, backing off his victim. Then he bowed with graceful formality, first to the woman, then to Engle.

Potter, gasping for breath and shaking his head as if trying to rid himself of the effects of his punishment, got slowly to his feet. When he had made it, the rest of the gunmen gave their full attention to Engle, who was unable to suppress a tight-lipped smile at the result of his threat. Then he stoked his anger and glared at the impassive Mexican.

"I asked for an explanation!"

"Sanchez can't talk, Mr. Engle," Burton supplied, tossing the Winchester back to its owner.

Steele raked his gaze over the expectant faces of the motley collection of professional gunmen. Even Potter looked eager behind the blood sheening his features. "At fifty dollars a day," he muttered to Conners, "money sure can."

CHAPTER THREE

Cliff Engle's wife was in her mid-twenties which made her about half his age. And there were a great many other differences between the couple. He was above average height with a stout build and a craggy face on which only expressions of anger or anxiety sat well. The texture of his skin showed that he had done much mannual work out of doors before he was able to afford expensive city clothing and the other luxuries of life after which Adam Steele hankered.

Felicity Engle was at least an inch under five feet in height and seemed almost fragilely slender. And she was very beautiful with jet black eyes and hair which emphasised the paleness of her skin. But she was obviously tougher than she looked for when she climbed gracefully out of the rear of the lead wagon there were no signs of weariness in her face or the way she moved.

Engle knew all about the trouble between Sanchez and Potter by then—the explanation delivered by Clint Burton to the accompaniment of curt nods from the mute Mexican. When the bloody-faced Potter tried again to make the excuse that he meant no harm, Engle swung around to yell at the wagon.

"Felicity, come on out of there!"

That was when his wife showed herself and it was apparent she had spent the time since arriving in Bradstock Landing in the feminine art of creating an impression. She was dressed in stylish riding breeches, boots buttoned to the knee and a short, body-hugging jacket. The whole outfit had been carefully brushed and she had also attended to her face and hair—removing the travel ravages of the long ride from New Orleans.

"Evening, gentlemen," she greeted with a bright smile as she came to a halt on the other side of the team from where her husband stood. Her dark eyes were attractively large and as they swept over the face of each gunman they seemed to imply her smile was especially for him.

All the men responded in a like manner but the Texans were particularly impressed, since her accent proved that she was from their home state. But only Marv Conners spoke.

"Howdy, ma'am."

Engle showed a mixture of anger and anxiety, although he had obviously known what the effect of his wife's appearance would be.

"My wife, you men!", he growled. "And I tell you now to remember that fact. You might also remember that before Felicity became Mrs. Engle her name was Meline."

Now he showed a tight-lipped smile as he drew another expected response. Steele was among those who reacted, for a man did not have to be a Texan to be aware of the wealth and reputation of Cole Meline.

"So I guess that's enough of a warning to you men," Engle continued. "Felicity's going to be with us all the way from here to Twin Creeks." He grimaced his distaste for the idea, then altered the expression hardly at all for a glance towards the assaulted woman who now stood unaided between her husband and brother-in-law. "And she's got more of what tempts a man than that . . ."

"Leave it, Clifford!" his wife cut in with a pitying

look at the other woman. Her tone was abrupt, angering Engle still more but not allowing him to ignore her. Then she rubbed salt in the wound. "Attend to your business."

She moved towards the woman, who backed off but then was won over by the sweet and apparently genuine smile of the daughter of one of the richest men in Texas. The two of them headed into the hotel, trailed by the hapless Pete. Rob went back into his café and the other local people withdrew into their houses.

"Let's get the cargo on board!" Engle snarled. "About time you men started earning the money I'm paying you!"

He made a wagon master's round arm gesture to set the train rolling and then strode out ahead of the lead team, down to the jetty and then along the bank to where the ancient stern-wheeler was moored. The gunmen ambled along at each side of the train, eyeing the wagons quizzically but drawing no clue as to what was concealed under the securely fastened canvas tops. The drivers stared directly ahead, tight-lipped and inviting no questions.

"Ridin' pretty high on the springs, Steele," Conners commented with a sage expression. "Funny how you always figure somethin' valuable oughta be heavy."

"The lady with the large eyes doesn't weigh more than a hundred pounds," the young Goldsmith said around a freshly lit cheroot as he glanced back over his shoulder. "But I'd put a high value on her."

"No higher than Engle, I'd say," Burton replied. "And Cole Meline must think highly of Engle to allow him into the family."

"Ain't nothin' to argue with in that, boy," Conners growled. "So best you take heed of what was told you about that high-breasted little Texas girl. I'd say she's trouble in a big way, wouldn't you, Steele?"

"We're already agreed, feller," the Virginian answered. "If it comes from Texas, it just has to be big."

Like the job he had been hired to do? And had accepted without knowing it had anything to do with land baron Cole Meline? Maybe if Steele had been aware of the Meline connection he would not have taken the down payment of fifty dollars and ridden north along the Mississippi to Bradstock Landing. For he was in New Orleans and lucky to be alive after a run-in with another rich and powerful family. A wilful and pretty daughter had been involved in that trouble, too. There had been no money, though. So Steele had been ready— even a little anxious—for a job when a nameless man with knowing eyes had approached him after a no-losers no-winners poker game.

Steele had seen the man before, during that first dry day after a week of warm, heavy rainfall: had sensed he was being studied rather than watched. There had been no feeling of impending danger. Just an awareness that the ordinary looking man had a strong sense of purpose and infinite patience.

"Your name's Adam Steele and that gun's like a third arm," had been his opening statement.

"It reaches further than the other two if needs be," the Virginian had answered.

A nod and the knowing eyes of the slightly built, middle-aged, smooth-skinned, untidily dressed man seemed to imply he had known what the answer would be before it was given. "I'm the agent of a man named Clifford Engle, Mr. Steele." He put a hand in a pants pocket and withdrew a sheaf of bills, with a bank band still around it. "There's fifty dollars here. To cover the time from now until you reach Bradstock Landing on Friday next. Don't matter when you get there, long as it's before sundown."

"After sundown on Friday?"

"Mr. Engle will be there by then. He'll answer all questions. Me and his other agents are just authorized to hire men like you, Mr. Steele."

"With guns like third arms?"

"And what it takes to use them." A knowing smile with the knowing eyes in which the mouth played no part. "If you ask questions, we are authorized to tell you this. At Bradstock Landing there will be a boat called *Queen of the River*. When Mr. Engle joins you, he'll have the cargo for the boat. Your job will be to guard that cargo on the trip to Twin Creeks which is a town just across the state line in Texas on the Red River. You'll get another fifty dollars at the end of each day during the trip."

"How many?"

"Days to Twin Creeks?"

"Men like me?"

"We are aiming for about ten."

There were twelve gunmen escorting the slow moving wagon train over the final few yards of its journey to the bank beside the moored sternwheeler. And although neither of them were now holding guns, the two men on board the *Queen* looked as tough and mean as any man ashore as they ran out a railed gangplank. Which brought the complement of guards up to fourteen.

Watching Engle's impatience while the gangplank was positioned between boat and bank, Steele recalled the final exchange of conversation between himself and the man in New Orleans.

"What happens if I take the fifty and don't show up at the landing, feller?"

"I'll remember you, Mr. Steele. And I'll have told others about you. It's not the money, you understand." He had spat then, scoring a direct hit into a tarnished brass cuspidor in the hotel lobby. "Fifty bucks is like that spit against all the water that comes down the Mis-

41

souri and Mississippi in a wet year. But it would be the principle." Another knowing smile. "I ain't just been looking at that rifle and the way you handle it, Mr. Steele. I've also been judging if you're a man of principle."

Now it was Marv Conners who spat, forcefully, to add his saliva to the river which was flowing sluggishly under the bright light of a three-quarter moon. "Will you look at that," he rasped.

"Niggers are valuable?" Goldsmith growled, bringing his boot heel down viciously on the glowing ash of his dropped cheroot.

The gangplank had been firmly rested on the bank and lashed to the rail of the sternwheeler. Engle had yelled an order and the wagon drivers had jumped to the ground and opened the flaps at the rear of their vehicles. Instructions liberally laced with obscenities had caused the human cargo to leave the wagons and form into a single file which shuffled towards the gangplank.

There were close to a hundred of them. All men in an age group spanning from eighteen to forty. Every one able-bodied and strong, dirty and unshaven but dressed identically in blue denim coveralls and stout work boots still retaining the stiffness of recent making. All of them were anxious as they surveyed their riverside surroundings and the blatant dislike which replaced surprise on almost every white face. Some made no attempt to mask their nervousness. Others tried to conceal it behind resentment and even arrogance.

"Engle!" Stan Clapham snarled. "Me and my kid brother ain't no nigger lovers. But we don't want nothin' to do with no slave runnin'!"

"And I sure as hell ain't gonna take no boat ride with this trash!" Vic Krantz bellowed, running the thong of his bullwhip through a fisted hand.

There was an undertone of malevolence in the buzz of talk that arose from the line of slow moving Negroes. And the denim garbed forms faltered in their steady progress along the bank and up the gangplank on to the boat.

"Keep moving!" Cliff Engle snapped. "You got my word and it's good!"

There was only a moment's hesitation before the line began to move freely again. Then Engle turned his full attention to the hired guns, who had formed into a single group beside the lead wagon.

"If you're that anti-black skin, Krantz, you can get the hell out of here!" he growled, striding towards the group. "And I don't want any refund. Because you came to where you were told." He halted and raked his hard eyes over every face turned towards him. "Same goes for any of you men who object to taking a boat trip with blacks. But hear this." He jerked a thumb over his shoulder. "These aren't slaves any more. They were when I bought them at an auction down in the Virgin Islands. But soon as I had them, I tore up the bill of sale and put them on the payroll. They aren't getting anything like what you men are being paid, but they're the same as you. Hired help. And I promised them they'll get treated the same as you?"

"Black niggers stink!" Krantz snarled.

"Not as much as corpses of any color!" Engle countered, glaring at the two-holstered gunman as viciously as Krantz glowered at the Negroes. "And any man that breaks my promise to these people will end up dead!"

"You ain't carryin', Engle!"

"But I am, you lippy bastard!" This from the red-haired, thickset, middle-aged man who had aimed a double barreled shotgun at Steele from the riverboat's wheelhouse. The gun had obviously been close at hand while he was helping position the gangplank. For he

43

had it again now, aimed from the shoulder. Over such a range, a blast from the twin muzzles would have peppered almost every man in the group.

Clint Burton showed his easy grin. "When a man has a dog, he doesn't have to bark himself."

"Just so, Burton," Engle said, proving again by his use of the right name for the right man that he had been fully informed about the help hired on his instructions. "And I can assure you men that Moran's bite is far worse than his bark."

"You pay good money, Mr. Engle," Will Breen said to cut through the last remnants of tension left from the objections of Krantz. "And personally I don't give a shit one way or the other whether these guys are slaves or not. But I'd sure like to know why I'm guardin' them. And from what."

Engle looked briefly at each man in turn once more. And gave a nod and a tight smile, expressing his satisfaction that only Krantz failed to show interest in what his answer would be. Then he even rubbed his hands together, after checking that almost all the Negroes were on board, squatting or stretching out full length on the main deck aft of the boiler.

"Understandable, Mr. Breen. The time for mystery is no more. But one thing, before I forget it. You used the word 'shit.' I can trade you obscenity for obscenity and not be upset by it. But if any man uses such language in earshot of my wife, he will answer to me." He jerked a thumb over his shoulder, but no one had to look towards the head of the gangplank to know that it would be Moran who would deal with miscreants.

"You make threats real fine, Mr. Engle," the young Sam Goldsmith muttered. "But we aren't . . ."

"The man's a high payer, boy," Conners cut in. "And at the rate he pays I'm willin' to listen to the rules he wants to make. Ain't you, Steele?"

Every time they had clashed eyes, Engle had made it plain he was not impressed by the Virginian, by a simple down turn at each corner of his mouth and a slight wrinkling of his nostrils. He did this again now—and spared part of the sneer for Conners, obviously contemptuous of the big Texan for valuing the opinion of the slightly built dude.

"He hasn't said anything yet I'm not prepared to go along with, feller."

Engle was about to spit, but a movement towards the rear of the parked wagons captured his attention and he swallowed his saliva. The bad taste stayed in his mouth. "Am I supposed to feel real good about that, Steele?" he growled as his wife neared the gangplank.

The Virginian shrugged. "A happy captain makes for a happy ship. But I don't reckon I was hired to spread goodwill, feller."

"None of us was," Ned McCall rasped. "What's at Twin Creeks and why d'we have to ride herd on the blacks gettin' there?"

Engle was still smarting over Steele's attitude, but his wife's presence held his temper in check. She had gone up the gangplank and was standing by the *Queen*'s forward deck rail, taking deep, regular breaths and smiling her enjoyment of the evening air over the river.

"All right, you men! We'll be leaving at sun-up tomorrow. But the watches will commence as soon as we board. Moran will draw up a duty roster. Reason you'll be guarding this ship and her passengers is that there's a group of troublemakers who aim to stop us getting to Twin Creeks."

"He sure talks a lot without sayin' a lot, don't he?" Conners murmured, not loud enough for Engle to hear.

But Cole Meline's son-in-law sensed the mounting impatience and hurried to reach his main point. "These men I'm taking upriver are strike breakers." He allowed

45

just a short pause, to give the gunmen time to react. But they gave nothing away by word or expression. "There are side issues but they need not concern you men. So I'll just tell you Mr. Meline plans to build a Texas-Kansas railroad and Twin Creeks is the base camp. The camp's built and supplies are stockpiled to start laying track north and south from the Red River. But there hasn't been a single tie put down since the bridge was put across the river. With these men from the Gulf islands me and Mr. Meline aim to change that situation."

"With a little help from us," Clint Burton added.

"Those of you who don't have sympathy for trouble-making strikers. And aren't prejudiced against colloreds."

His first condition was accepted without response. The second caused everyone to look at Vic Krantz. The short-necked man scowled up at the Negroes huddled on the deck of the riverboat and touched one side of his Mexican-style moustache with the bullwhip. And grinned.

"Hell, it only takes one hand to use a whip or a sixshooter, Mr. Engle. Leaves the other one free to hold my nose."

Engle nodded, obviously pleased to have the brawny, tough-talking Krantz along. "Anybody else want out for any reason?"

The sneering look towards Steele again, this time perhaps indicating a wish that the Virginian would take offense at his attitude.

"Not me, feller," Steele replied evenly with an easy grin towards the Negro islanders. "I've got nothing against men who want to go to work. Color of their legs makes no difference."

CHAPTER FOUR

Will Breen's luck ran out at three o'clock in the morning. And neither Ned McCall nor Duke Fargo were to blame for the bullet which drilled into the Texan's right eye and tunnelled through his brain before it was impacted into the inside of his skull.

It had been a peaceful night until Breen shouted the warning which invited the bullet. The first four hour watch had ended at midnight and Breen, Krantz, Conners and Steele were three-quarters of the way through their guard duty. The moon was still in evidence but its light was dimmed by a blanket of low cloud which threatened a downpour of warm rain. The crude buildings of Bradstock Landing were in total darkness. So were the wagons with their drivers sleeping beneath them, the men resting up before starting the trip back to New Orleans in the morning. On board the *Queen of the River* there was a pool of light from two kerosene lamps hung above the boiler's firebox. This illuminated Moran and the blond youngster—whose name was Campbell—as they laid kindling and cordwood in the box.

The two rivermen did not talk and they made little other noise as they built the fire. Negroes and white men snored and grunted in their sleep as they slumbered on the open main deck or in the cabins between the hurricane and boiler decks. Occasionally one of the

47

oxen, free of the wagon traces but hobbled by the fore-legs in a lush grass meadow, would low. The Mississippi gurgled around the hull of the sternwheeler, the sound constant enough to be almost hypnotic. Boot leather scraped against decking as the sentries patrolled their stations, trying to remain alert in the dark, quiet hours of a new day's pre-birth.

The attackers reached the fore and aft mooring lines, hitched around heavy stakes driven into the bank, be-cause they came from an unexpected quarter. Two of the teamsters crawled out from under their wagons and then went down on to their bellies to cover the final feet. Breen in the bow, Conners at the stern and Steele and Krantz fore and aft of the wheelhouse were concen-trating their attention beyong the immediate vicinity of the riverboat, seeking to spot intruders before they came close enough to do damage. Their eyes were rak-ing the meadows, brush and timber on the east side of the river, scanning the far bank and switching first one way and then the other to survey the unruffled surface of the slow moving Mississippi.

The two wagon drivers, knives in one hand and re-volvers in the other, were in moon shade of the *Queen* as they squatted beside the stakes and began to saw at the stout, taut mooring lines.

Moran straightened up from crouching in front of the firebox and hit his temple hard against one of the hang-ing lamps. He cursed with low venom, glaring hatefully at the swinging lantern. The area of light lengthened and contracted rhythmically. And Will Breen did a dou-ble take as a glint of light refracted off metal caught his eye.

"Hold it right there!" the Texan known for his fair fighting yelled. He whirled sideways to the man on the bank, drew, cocked and levelled his Colt, but stayed his forefinger on the trigger.

48

It was the glint ot the knife blade which had attracted Breen's attention. And the Texan was unaware of the revolver in the teamster's other hand until he saw the muzzle flash and heard the report of an expended bullet. The lucky shot, fired fast on an upwards trajectory, blasted into Breen's head and folded him backwards over the top of the steam capstan.

"The bastards are here!" Krantz roared as he and the other guards lunged for the port deck edge, cocked guns raking back and forth as narrowed eyes sought a target.

The bow line parted with a sharp crack almost as loud as the gunshot which had preceded it. The stern rope groaned under the additional strain as the river sought to wrench the powerless boat free of restraint.

Breen's killer leapt to his feet and yelled something to his partner as he exploded a second shot.

The bullet missed Krantz by several feet and smashed a window in the wheelhouse. Only the gunshot and crash of shattered glass could be heard distinctly above the cacophony of other noise as rudely awakened men on the boat and shore cursed and yelled demands to know what was happening.

Krantz, Conners and Steele fired in unison. The man who had killed Breen staggered backwards on legs which seemed made of rubber. Blood was pumping from the center of his chest, through the hole drilled by Krantz's bullet.

The man at the stern of the boat had failed to sever the line. He was driven by panic to give up the task, whip erect, turn and race towards the closest patch of cover—which was the group of oxen. He had taken no more than three long strides when two bullets struck him. The one from Conner's Remington sank deep into his right thigh. Steele's shot smashed into the man's left leg behind the knee, the power of the rifle boosting it all

49

the way through and smashing the bone cap as it exited.

If the man screamed as he went down, his revolver spinning far out of his hand, the sound of his agony was masked by deep throated shouts, and the roar of twin barrels expending their loads of shot.

Abruptly there was a brittle silence broken only by water running around the hull of the sternwheeler. It lasted for no longer than two seconds as those with a view of the scene stared at the blood-soaked, shot-torn body of the man who had cut the bow line, and those who could not see sensed the presence of violent death.

The moon found a hold in the cloud and punched a shaft of bright light earthwards. Tiny red bubbles of blood foam burst and the humped form of the dead man on the bank appeared to be covered with a smooth, sheened, scarlet blanket.

Moran, braced against the side of the boiler, broke open his shotgun to eject the empty cartridges. He fed in fresh loads with the deft speed of an expert.

The man who had tried to run was now inching forward on his stomach, hauling himself along with his hands on tufts of grass. His legs trailed uselessly behind him. Perhaps delirious and unaware that he was bathed in bright moonlight, he sank his teeth deep into his lower lip, fighting to control the screams of agony that were demanding to be released.

Steele could not see Moran, but he recognized the sounds of the shotgun being broken, loaded and snapped shut.

"You hit a man when he's down and you'll likely seal his lips, feller!" the Virginian shouted. "For ever!"

Voices sounded again on the boat and on shore. But they were low. Men were running towards the scene of the shooting from Bradstock Landing. Lamplight shone from the windows and doorways of the buildings behind them. The teamsters were out from under their wagons and huddled into a tight-knit group which seemed to emanate a quality of fear.

"You ain't along to give with the orders, little man!" Moran rasped, recognising Steele's unmistakable Virginia drawl. "You and the rest of this bunch supposed to be hotshots with shootin' irons. Yet I gotta finish off your work for you!"

"Hold your fire, Moran!" Engle bellowed down from the companionway linking the two upper decks. "And secure this ship!"

Engle's angry voice brought silence again, except for heavy footfalls against decking as Moran and Campbell moved to replace the severed and damaged mooring lines and the gunmen formed into groups around the dead and injured.

Steele remained where he was at the side of the wheelhouse, paying scant attention to the activity. Instead he continued his interrupted survey of the river and its banks, watching with war trained eyes for the first sign of a new attack to back up the abortive first one. But nothing moved out there except the relentless flow of the Mississippi.

"You aimed for his leg, didn't you, Steele?" Marv Conners growled irritably as he reached the top of the open stairway from the hurricane deck. He came to stand beside and tower above the Virginian. But he didn't look at Steele. Instead, he gazed disconsolately towards where Engle, the Clapham brothers, Potter and Burton were gathered around the man with useless legs. The man had screamed, once, when a boot had been hooked under his belly to flip him over on to his back.

"Not you, feller?" Steele replied.

"I ain't that good. Not any more. It's like that snot-nose city kid gettin' the drop on me. Few years back I'd have put a bullet between his eyes before he even thought about makin' a play. Same as I'd have plugged that guy plumb in the middle of his back. Where I was aimin' at."

The Virginian glanced at the grim set profile of the disenchanted Texan. "I've been told I've got a sympathetic face, feller," he said. "But my shoulders aren't for crying on."

"So go to hell." He said it softly and did not move his feet or the direction of his gaze. "Don't you ever need someone to listen to you sometimes?"

"No, feller. I worked it out on my own. If I find out I'm no good at something, I stop doing it."

Conners sighed and rasped the knuckles of a tight fist over his jaw bristles. "That's okay if a man ain't too proud to be smart."

"The bastard killed Will!"

It was Ned McCall who made the shouted announcement, looking up towards Steele and Conners as he backed down the gangplank. He was holding the ankles of the dead Texan while Fargo gripped the corpse under the armpits.

"Never figured it'd happen that way," Conners answered indifferently.

"Hey, Mr. Engles!" one of the teamsters roared. "We ain't all tarred with the same brush!"

There was bitter complaint in his tone as he and his grim-faced companions were covered by the guns of Goldsmith, Krantz and Ricardo Sanchez. But they had controlled their feelings until Engle started back towards the gangplank, trailed by the Claphams and Potter and Burton. The bearded brothers had charge of the prisoner, dragging him face down by the outstretched arms. The injured man had strength enough only to groan as his shattered kneecap bumped over the uneven ground.

"Then you have nothing to worry about!" Engle growled, continuing to stride along the bank until he reached the shot-blasted body of Breen's killer. "But I'll be real anxious until I'm sure."

The prisoner was released, but he was only able to flop out full-length on the trampled grass of the bank and turn his head so that he was not staring into the heap of torn and bloodied flesh that had once been his partner. In the moon and lamp light the terror inscribed on his face was clear to see. It was the face of a forty-year-old, thin and angular with deep set eyes and a prominent nose. The skin was pale under the dirt and bristles.

"Moran, get over here!" Engle ordered, then moderated his tone as he looked up at the companionway below where Steele and Conners stood. "It would be better if you returned to the cabin, Felicity, my dear."

"I'd rather stay outside, Cliff," his wife answered.

There was no determination in her voice and it was again obvious that Mrs. Engle was a woman accustomed to getting her own way without undue effort.

"Just as you wish," her husband rasped through lips pursed in a frown, then put his back to the boat and spoke in low tones to Moran.

The thick-set, red-headed crewman was carrying his shotgun again now that he and Campbell had secured the sternwheeler with new lines fore and aft. He nodded several times, trying not to grin, as he was given his instructions. Then he thrust the gun at Campbell. The youngster seemed afraid of it until he had carefully pushed the twin hammers back to the rest.

The men standing close to Moran and the prisoner backed off several steps. The male members of the family who operated Bradstock Landing came closer for a better view. The drivers and the trio of gunmen covering them shifted position so that they all could see. The Negroes jostled one another to the same end. The river once more became the only source of sound.

53

"How many more like you?" Engle demanded.

The injured man was no longer delirious. Ever since he had been dropped beside the dead man his awareness of his position had sharpened. And his fear had expanded. His eyes had been constantly moving in their sockets, shifting from one group of watchers to the other. Until his attention was captured by McCall and Fargo. They were furthest away from him, under a sycamore tree in the centre of the lush meadow beside which the sternwheeler was moored. The stiffening corpse of Will Breen was out of sight in the long grass. Soon he would be hidden for all time, in the grave which McCall and Fargo were digging with shovels they had taken from two of the wagons.

The men wielding the shovels seemed oblivious to what was happening on the river bank. And the prisoner appeared to be trying to achieve a similar state of mind. Knowing that soon he would need a grave. Wishing, perhaps, that he was already dead.

"Poor bastard," Conners hissed.

The man had not heard the question.

Moran took a backward step, then one to the side. He balanced his bulky frame, drew back a leg and kicked it forward.

Conners winced and Felicity Engle gasped. Many others reacted in a similar way as Moran's booted foot arced down between the helplessly splayed legs of his victim and smashed into his crotch.

The man screamed. High and loud and long. Pressing his body and face hard against the ground and clawing his hands at the grass. As if trying to escape this new agony by burying himself. Then his voice broke with a sob.

"Mr. Engle asked how many more like you and your buddy!" Moran snarled.

He had moved again, and now dropped to his

haunches, to bunch a handful of the man's hair and jerk up his head.

"It was that ape should have been killed," Conners muttered. "Not Will Breen."

Steele was showing no reaction to the brutality happening down on the bank. And his impassive face was a true reflection of his total lack of feeling. He had accepted money from Engle to do a job and thus owed his allegiance to the man who was paying him. Whether he approved or otherwise of Engle's methods was immaterial. It mattered only that the terrified and suffering man forced to stare into the cruel face of Moran was an enemy of the group the Virginian had joined.

The violent peace had been filled with situations such as this and Steele no longer had consciously to apply the principles of war to them. His code was as natural to him as breathing. And for the most part as automatic.

"You reckon Moran's unique, feller?" Steele asked as the agonised man below opened and closed his mouth, trying to force out a reply.

Conners, still grimacing his distaste for what was happening, allowed his gaze to wander over the faces of the other hired guns. Without exception, they were enjoying the brutal spectacle—even envious of Moran's part in it.

He shook his head, sad-faced now. "You're right, Steele. And I'm wrong for this job. Hearin' what men are like ain't the same as seein' them operate, is it?"

The prisoner was still flapping his mouth without getting any words out. Engle vented a grunt of impatience. Moran rose into a half crouch and dragged his victim by the hair. The man found voice to scream again as he was lifted higher—then had his face pushed down against the shot-ravaged belly of the dead teamster. He made gagging, retching noises as his face was ground into the torn flesh. The coating of congealed blood was

55

broken and the moist redness beneath was transferred from dead to living skin.

Moran jerked on the hair again, and brought a foot into play to turn the prisoner over on his back. Vomit gushed from the mouth, erupting upwards and then splashing down to spread even more ghastly areas of colour over the blood-spread face.

"You're gettin' the idea!" Moran crowed, and vented a short gust of obscene laughter as the punished man wrenched his head to one side and choked up the last remnants of half digested food from his stomach. "Mr. Engle wants you to spill your guts!"

"I advised you not to watch this!" Engle called up to his wife. The unhealthy pallor of his skin suggested he was feeling sick himself. And it was obvious he was reluctant to return his attention to the brutalized man after finding an excuse to look away from him.

"I am making no complaint, Cliff," the woman replied without emotion.

"Quiet!" Moran roared, dropping on to his haunches again and cocking his head to one side.

His stomach empty, and safe from choking, the prisoner was looking directly up at the sky which was now completely clear of cloud immediately overhead. The first sounds he made were gibberish, but then he started to form words. Slowly and painfully.

"There . . . was . . . just . . . me . . . and . . . Fred. We ain't . . . we ain't . . . part of . . . of . . . nothin'. We just talked . . . it over and we reckoned it wasn't right. What you're doin'. Bringin' in niggers to take . . . to take the bread outta white men's mouths. Outta the mouths of their families . . . their kids."

"You expect Mr. Engle to . . ."

"Shut up, Moran!" Engle snarled, and moved in closer to crouch beside the torturer and tortured. Even

56

though it was easy to hear the man's words in the almost total silence of the pre-dawn hours.

"That's the honest truth, I swear it," the man continued, stringing his words closer together now. "Me and Fred, we got wives and kids ourselves. We're just workin' men like them up at Twin Creeks. We ain't gunslingers like them you hired. Didn't figure to kill nobody. Just to cut the boat loose. Hoped she'd drift on to a spit. Smash her wheel on a snag, maybe."

"And leave us sitting ducks for Garrett guns?" Engle growled.

"Me and Fred don't . . . didn't know nothin' about any Garrett," came the fast, anxious reply. "We was on our own. I swear that. By everythin's holy, Mr. Engle."

The crouching forms of Engle and Moran blocked the man's face to all other eyes. But his voice, beginning to waver again, held a strong ring of truth.

Engle stood up.

"You want me to finish him off?" Moran asked eagerly, rising and turning, holding out his hands to take back his shotgun from Campbell.

"You did as much as I needed from you!" Engle snapped. "Fire up the boiler! Soon as we've got a head of steam, we'll leave! You men, turn the drivers free. They can bury the dead one and take this man back to the city with them!" He raised his voice to shout louder. "You local people, get back to your beds! Anyone not in my employ who comes within fifty feet of this boat will be shot!"

He whirled and strode back towards the gangplank. Moran and Campbell were ahead of him, moving fast to obey their orders.

"Except for the feller named Hank," Steele called down.

Engle came to an abrupt halt to glare up at the Virginian. He was in the grip of a deep rage which seemed

57

somehow contrived—an easily erected shield to conceal his true emotion. Which was fear or shame. Maybe a combination of the two.

"The ferryman has no business aboard the *Queen of the River*! You heard my order!"

"He's got business with me, feller. We have some horse-trading to do."

"Then you move your ass down off the boat and go see him, Steele. And hear this: I won't lose no sleep if you don't get back on board again."

"Best you keep your mouth shut when you don't know what you're talking about, Cliff," his wife advised tonelessly from the companionway. Her words dug the lines of the angry frown deeper into his fleshy face. "From what I've been overhearing up here it's the gentleman with him who isn't up to this job."

Marv Conners formed the word "bitch" with his narrow lips, but did not speak it. Instead: "I just ain't for beatin' up a helpless man, Mr. Engle."

Engle's anger was completely genuine now, aroused by his wife's dominance of him. Spittle sprayed from his mouth when he snapped it open to direct an angry retort at the Texan. But he choked on his humiliation and didn't trust himself to shout.

"Damn it, I knew I should have picked the men myself!" he rasped, and clambered fast up the gangway.

"I heard tell you'd turned yellow, Conners!" Ned McCall growled as he and Fargo neared the sternwheeler, their burying chore ended. "Will said he didn't believe it."

"What Will Breen said or believed don't matter no more," the big Texan answered dully, declining to accept the insult as Steele moved aft and started down the stairway to the lower deck.

"Sure thing. But what you are could matter to us in a tight spot."

This got to Conners. He narrowed his eyes, set his jaw in a firm line and pulled back his shoulders. All activity on and in the vicinity of the sternwheeler abruptly ceased attention was captured by the threat of further violence. "That because your keeper's dead, McCall?"

The man on the bank had adopted the same gunfighter's stance and pasted a similar inscrutable expression on his dirt-streaked, heavily stubbled face.

The only thing that moved apart from the Mississippi was the Virginian, strolling nonchalantly along the companionway towards the hurricane deck. He tried to ignore the woman's perfume as he neared where she stood against the rail. It was impossible not to be aware of the beauty of her silhouette—face and body.

"Frig it, you men!" Engle roared. "There'll be plenty of trouble from other quarters before we reach Twin Creeks!"

"I ain't anxious to prove nothin' right now," Conners drawled.

"Nor ain't Ned," Duke Fargo said quickly, stepping to the side to place himself between McCall and Conners. He had to clench his hands into fists to keep them from trembling with the strain.

Felicity Engle released her own inner tension with a soft sigh as she turned her head to look at the Virginian.

"You're a real hard man, aren't you, Adam Steele?" she asked as aboard and ashore others moved to continue their interrupted chores.

He had the rifle canted to his left shoulder. He touched the brim of his hat with his right hand. "Understand that was the kind your husband wanted, ma'am."

She nodded. "But you're not the kind to indulge in pretence of any sort. Like those two fools." She tossed her head to indicate Conners above her. Then moved it to the side to direct a scornful glance at McCall. Her

59

long hair swayed, releasing more of the fragrance of her perfume. "The kind that are never sure of themselves. So they always have to be proving what they think they are."

"Felicity!" Engle snapped as he crossed the hurricane deck after climbing the main stairway. "Is this man annoying you?"

He has his right hand in a pocket, perhaps fisted around the butt of a small gun.

"No, Cliff," she replied, matching his tone. "And after being married to you for three years I guess I ought to know!"

She whirled, crossed the companionway, went through the open doorway of her cabin and slammed the door closed behind her.

Engle was embarrassed by the outburst. For a moment he was dumbstruck. Then he tried to contrive a fresh display of anger. But he was too physically and emotionally exhausted for the effort it required.

"It's been a rough day," he said at length, unable to hold Steele's steady gaze. "Felicity isn't herself."

"You're paying me to do a job, feller," Steele told him evenly, moving on past the weary-eyed, stoop-shouldered man. "Not to listen to you tell lies."

CHAPTER FIVE

The *Queen of the River* left her mooring place just as the eastern dome of the sky was beginning to shade from black into grey with the approaching dawn. Dark, aromatic wood smoke belched from her twin stacks and the big sternwheel thrashed the mud-colored water to white foam. Steam hissed from escape valves and her engines throbbed. Her ancient and ill-cared-for hull and superstructure trembled with the power of the brand new machinery which drove her.

Engle was in the wheelhouse, Moran fired the boiler and Campbell tended the engine. Each of them was skilled in his particular job and the boat was eased away from the bank, turned in midstream and headed upriver with smooth and unhurried professionalism.

"These guys know what they're about," Frank Potter said with admiration in his eyes. "I used to ride the Missouri boats a lot."

"So they know about stinkin' boats!" Krantz growled. "What the hell do we know about them?"

"Cole Meline's backin' Engle," Stan Clapham drawled. "Good enough for me."

"Likewise," his younger brother agreed.

"Who's Garrett?" Duke Fargo asked, looking at Conners.

All eleven guards were on the hurricane deck, leaning or sitting on the rails. Some were smoking, adding the scent of burning tobacco to the early morning air already filled with the pleasant smells of woodsmoke and cooking meat. They had congregated there after returning from the landing office where Hank Bradstock had driven hard bargains for their horses. No man had sold his gear and it was now all piled in the center of the deck.

By the time they returned to the sternwheeler Cliff Engle had designated a top man among the Negroes and issued him orders. So breakfast was already being prepared in the galley and there was ample black labor taking care of the other menial and unskilled chores aboard.

Thus, the gunmen got their first taste of feeling inadequate and bored as they watched in idleness as the *Queen of the River* was cast off and brought about to start the trip north.

Steele underwent the same experience as the rest but had the temperament to accept his lot with equanimity. Glancing around at the others he recognised that the mute Sanchez and cultured Burton were also men of infinite patience. The rest were on edge. Men of action who needed activity or excitement in liberal doses. At the landing there had been liquor and strangers and anticipation of the job to come to occupy these men. Then the trouble between Potter and the Mexican, the arrival of Engle with the blacks, and the attempted sabotage of the boat with the violence that accompanied it.

Appetites had been whetted for more of the same. There was tension in the air—low keyed at this early stage—which could be relieved by talk.

"How the hell should I know?" Conners snapped, and this waspish response from the usually easy-going Texan was symptomatic of the mood in general of most of the men lounging on the forward deck.

"You always claimed to know everythin' about every man carries a gun," Ned McCall countered.

"From Texas," Conners corrected, moderating his tone, anxious not to rekindle the fires of trouble with the bullet-scarred man. "Either Garret ain't from Texas or he ain't no pro with a gun."

"I guess Engle would have told us. if he thought we needed to know," Sam Goldsmith growled through teeth clenched on a fresh cheroot.

Whenever the skinny, city-dressed youngster spoke or even made a move, the gold-flecked dark eyes of Vic Krantz would flick hatefully towards him. Confirming yet another potential explosion of violence between two men hired to fight on the same side.

"I can't see how it matters," Clint Burton said to end a lengthening silence as the first shaft of bright yellow light from the rising sun lanced across the lushness of Louisiana. "If he was something real special, I guess we'd have heard of him. Wouldn't you say that, Steele?"

Everyone turned their attention towards the Virginian, who was leaning across the rail on the starboard side, looking back along the side of the boat and through the spray from the paddlewheel to where the buildings of Bradstock Landing diminished in perspective.

Steele glanced over his shoulder at the men and saw indifference to him on most faces. Marv Conners still accepted him as an equal, or perhaps even better than that. Burton respected him. Ned McCall was warily resentful as he remembered the incident on the jetty.

"They say a picture's worth a thousand words, feller," Steele answered.

"You ain't said more than hundred since we tied in together, dude," Stan Clapham muttered.

"And them you do say ain't exactly as plain as the sun in the friggin' sky," his brother added.

"Steele means words can say anything," Burton amplified. "So the only way to find out what a man's really like is to see him in action."

The Mexican nodded his agreement.

Conners pointed at Sanchez and grinned. "You all seen him in action." Then he became grim faced as he flicked his gaze between McCall and Fargo. "Few of us seen Steele operate. I wouldn't like to have to go up against either one of them when the chips were down."

Two skillets were clacked together down on the lower aft deck. The a deep voice bellowed: "Grub up! Come and get it!"

"I ain't eatin' with no niggers!" Krantz snarled, running the thong of the bullwhip through a clenched fist.

"So friggin' starve," Goldsmith muttered malevolently, and started for the head of the main stairway.

Krantz uttered an animalistic roar, unclenched his left fist and threw his right arm forward. The leather cracked against the air, the tip of the thong more than two feet away from where Goldsmith had come to an abrupt halt. But it was a deliberate miss. For Krantz saw that the boy's Colt was clear of the holster, cocked and aimed—and he pulled his arm in against his chest.

The skinny youngster uncocked the revolver and thrust it firmly back in his holster. Then parted his lips and grinned around the cheroot clenched in his teeth. "Just testing you," he said, flicking the underside of his derby brim in an arrogant gesture. "So you'll know I've got the beating of you if you start something."

"You reckon that's what those fellers trailing us are doing?" Steele asked, capturing the surprised looks away from Krantz and Goldsmith. "Testing us?"

Ricardo Sanchez had been sharing the Virginian's interest in the group of horsemen moving relentlessly along the eastern bank of the river. Six of them, cantering their mounts to maintain an unwavering gap of half a mile between themselves and the sternwheeler. The Mexican gave Steele a hard stare and a curt nod, then pumped the action of his Winchester as all the men on the hurricane deck moved to the rail and leaned across it to peer astern of the *Queen of the River*.

"Hey, ain't they . . ." Duke Fargo began.

"Fellers from the landing," Steele cut in to confirm. "Except for the one who runs the café."

"Ridin' our horses, frig it!" Potter growled.

The boat's steam whistle shrilled. Short and loud, like the call of some large bird in distress.

"Engle's spotted 'em," Krantz said as the predetermined danger signal was curtailed.

"Or maybe it's that has got him worried," Burton answered, pointing upriver.

All attention was switched in that direction and with the exception of the Virginian and the Mexican all the men moved to line up along the forward deck rail.

The sternwheeler was veering to port, staying in midstream as the river made a wide, sweeping curve to the left. The turn of the Mississippi was almost a complete half circle, cutting between lush, green meadows before its sun-glinting surface went from sight in a broad stand of timber. On the fringe of the wood the trees were widely spaced and it was possible to see another riverboat. A sidewheeler, half the size of the *Queen*. Her single stack was giving off little smoke and she was moving very slowly, as if the drive to her paddles was disconnected and she was simply drifting on the seaward flow of the river.

"You reckon we're about to start earning our money, feller?" Steele asked Sanchez, lowering the Colt Hartford to rest the barrel on the deck rail. He thumbed back the hammer.

The smile on the good looking face of the Mexican appeared charming at first glance. But his dark eyes were as lifeless as black pebbles as he pumped the action of the Winchester again. It was not a mistake. For he was ready for the live bullet to be ejected. A long arm was curved out, hand splayed. He caught the spinning shell neatly and fed it back through the rifle's loading gate: the whole a part of a single, smooth movement. Then he made a circle with a thumb and forefinger before he gripped the rifle two-handed, angled across the front of his body.

Another steam whistle howled.

Smoke belched from the stack of the sidewheeler. It formed an ominous black cloud among the trees. Then she surged forward, paddles beating the water to white foam.

Hank, Pete, Hank's three sons and a stranger yelled at their horses and thudded heels against flanks to spurt the animals into a gallop.

Perhaps because he knew he was dealing with individualists—or maybe because he simply had not expected more trouble this early—Engle had neglected to issue specific instructions as to what his hired guns should do after he sounded the danger signal.

Steele was first to move, pushing away from the rail and turning to start along the companionway for the boiler deck aft of the cabins. Other footfalls rapped against the decking behind him. He snatched a look over his shoulder and saw Sanchez was hard on his heels. Behind him was Marv Conners, Remington drawn. Then Clint Burton, hand under his jacket.

"What's happening?" Felicity Engle demanded. She was still tousled from sleep, but looked good despite her lack of face paint and powder and her dishevelled hair. Her body was encased in a flame red dressing gown, belted at the waist but showing the lacy frills of a black nightdress around her legs and hiding her torso.

"All kinds of trouble if you come outside your cabin

66

dressed in that outfit, ma'am," Steele rasped at her as he ran across the deck to the rail above the whirling paddlewheel.

The woman, who advanced as far as the end of the port companionway, glowered at Steele, then looked down at herself. When she looked up again, she saw that the Virginian and Mexican were ignoring her. But that Conners and Burton had slowed their advance on the stern—to pay more attention to her with eager eyes than to the galloping horsemen on the bank.

"Shit!" she hissed. "Don't men ever think of anything else!" Then she whirled and hurried back to her cabin.

Conners and Burton joined Steele and Sanchez at the rail, bunched to the left of the starboard toilet. The door of the privy was flung open and a scared looking Negro came out, still fixing the front fastening of his denim coveralls.

"What's happenin', man?" he gasped.

"Prayin' time," Burton told him.

"On account you can't do nothin' else without a gun, black man!" Conners added.

The Negro stared back at the racing horsemen and bobbed his head in agreement. "I sure hope you fellers is as good as Mr. Engle said you'd be," he yelled, and went at a run across the deck and down the iron ladder to the lower deck.

Puffs of white smoke showed against the dark of horses and riders. The sound of the gunshots reached the ears of the men aboard the sternwheeler at the same time as the thud of bullets impacting with wood.

"There are guns and guns, I'd say," Burton rasped as he pulled a tiny, pearl-handled Smith and Wesson .32 from his shoulder holster and looked from it to the Remington in Conners's hand.

Steele squeezed the trigger of the Colt Hartford. The

67

Mexican was a split second later in exploding a shot from his Winchester.

Two of Hank's sons threw their arms high in the air. One toppled immediately from the saddle, falling to the side and causing the man beside him to veer violently to the right. The other tried to hold on. But blood from his punctured chest spurted over the neck of his mount. The animal responded to the spray of warm moisture by trying to rear at the gallop. The rider was flipped backwards from the saddle. The hindlegs of the horse could not take the strain and splayed apart on the marshy grass. Then the animal crashed down on to its side with neck stretched and legs flailing.

Pete's horse tried to leap the fallen mount and rider. But a trailing hoof smashed into the raised head of the horse struggling on the ground. Balance was lost and the leaping horse tipped to the side in mid-air. Pete made the mistake of trying to jump clear: releasing his hold on the reins and kicking free of the stirrups.

His horse bucked to gain height—and the rider was catapulted forward. He hit the ground head first. It was soft ground, which gave under his weight. But the earth was compacted and held the man's head in a firm grip as his body and limbs were hurled forward by momentum.

Although distance made it impossible, the men at the stern of the *Queen of the River* seemed to hear the dry crack as Pete's neck snapped a moment before his lifeless torso and legs slammed to the turf.

His horse and the other two riderless mounts— recovered from the effects of two rifle bullets— continued to gallop flat out along the river bank. One mounted rider chased them, maintaining control with heels and knees as he used both hands to pump and fire a repeating rifle.

Hank and his uninjured son reined their horses to a

68

skidding halt, wheeled them and headed back the way they had come to leap from their saddles as they came close to where three inert forms were sprawled on the bank.

The stranger chasing the riverboat almost got lucky. One of his bullets glanced off an arcing blade of the paddlewheel and spun close enough to Burton's cheek to cause the Bostonian to yell in alarm.

Steele and Sanchez squeezed off two shots that sounded as one. And the horseman was close enough to the boat now for his expression of surprise to be clearly seen as he reacted to the lead burrowing into his flesh. He looked down at himself, saw the two patches of crimson on his chest, and raised his head again. His mouth was gaping now. So wide that the lips seemed folded back far enough to use every square inch of his face to power the scream.

He tried to bring his horse to a halt, but his right arm was paralysed and every ounce of his remaining strength was applied through his left arm. The horse veered across the bank, lost its footing in panic when the river came directly ahead, and plunged into the water. Man and mount tipped over. The horse found footing on the mud in the shallows under the bank and scrambled up on to dry land. Then the man surfaced, face down and moving only because the Mississippi was never inert.

"But ain't no one needs to pray, Yank," Conners drawled, sliding the Remington back into the holster. "Seems the Lord has already provided."

The grins which he and Burton directed towards Steele and Sanchez were suddenly frozen for an instant. For a sound like a single thunderclap drowned all else. And then horror replaced easy good humor as a high-pitched whistle filled the warming, gunsmoke-stinking air of the new day.

69

"Sonofabitches, they got them a mortar!" Conners snarled.

He was the last of the quartet on the boiler deck to go down. And only then was sent sprawling by Sanchez curling an arm around his knees and thudding a shoulder into his calves.

The shell hit. It smashed through the yawl slung above the rail on the port side of the boiler deck, then went through the deck board beneath. To the men close by, the sound of the double impact was louder than the explosion of the detonating powder. Splinters of wood were sprayed with lethal force across the open deck, but too high to harm the four gunmen pressed hard to the boards.

"Sonsofbitches, Mr. Conners," Clint Burton said in the stretched seconds of silence which followed the deafening effects of the mortar shot. "If you're going to get a beating for foul language, use the right term."

There was not a real silence, of course. The *Queen of the River* and the second boat continued to thrash the Mississippi to angry whiteness and their engines, pushed to full power, clattered and whined as if seeking to break loose from their mountings. But the men on the aft top deck seemed to be in a private world of their own sounds as their ears buzzed an impenetrable barrier against all noises beyond their immediate sphere of existence. But, as if in deliberate compensation, it seemed like they could see with more clarity than ever before. Colors appeared very bright and shapes were sharply placed one upon the other.

Steele was familiar with this sensation of unreality in a time of extreme danger. Probably many of the other men aboard the speeding riverboat had also experienced it before, whether at the height of a full scale battle during the war, or during a gunfight not yet decided. It was a feeling that descended upon a man when he knew he had escaped death—by part of a second or a fraction of an inch. The clarity of vision and awareness of individual sounds through a great confusion of noise amounted to a man's involuntary appreciation of the life he had almost lost.

It was something akin to euphoria. And it was insinuatingly dangerous: for a man could easily allow himself to be lulled into a sense of false security as he indulged the sensations of well-being.

Conners, Burton and Sanchez were as aware of the risks as the Virginian.

Nobody had to say anything and there was not even an exchange of looks. They rose in unison and raced for the port companionway.

The sights and sounds of the world were blurred and distorted again. Below their feet the boat shruddered under the strain of full power. The banks of the river were indistinct patches of green and brown and black in many shades. Peaceful countryside of no interest because the danger it held was no longer a threat.

The men heard the engines and the paddlewheel. Gunfire and shouts. Bullets thudding into timber and ricocheting off metal.

"Sonofabitch!" Conners snarled, skidding to a halt as he led the other three on to the hurricane deck. "He crazy?"

"At singular curses there's nothing he needs to learn, Mrs. Engle," Burton said, breathlessness detracting from his cultured Boston accent.

The woman, hurriedly dressed in the expensive riding breeches and jacket, was peering ahead from the cover of the port smokestack. There was excitement in her black eyes and her breasts rose and fell in rapid time against the tightness of her jacket. But she controlled herself and her tone was even as she looked at the men.

"Do not be fooled by appearances, gentleman. In this situation, Cliff knows what he is doing."

What her husband was doing was not designed to inspire confidence in the men aboard the *Queen of the River*. For he was maintaining full speed from the engines as he veered the sternwheeler to port. To hold a collision course with the other riverboat which had swung to starboard.

Both boats were heeled over by the speed and suddenness of their turns.

A second mortar shell was hurled through the morning air on a low trajectory, but the change of course and tilt of the sidewheeler's deck ruined the gunner's aim. And the shell cracked from the gun in front of the wheelhouse and whistled its useless way into the shallows under the west bank of the river.

The loader made to pick up another shell. But the gunner had already fled his position: he was racing along the deck beside the wheelhouse for the aft stairway. His partner abandoned the heap of shells and chased after him.

Covering fire was sprayed towards the *Queen of the River* by at least six riflemen spread out along the port side of the sidewheeler. Puffs of white muzzle smoke pinpointed the positions of the men. Their bullets hit the sternwheeler. But the crack of shots and the thud of impacting bullets were masked by roaring engines, thrashing paddles and the continuous howl of a steam whistle.

The sidewheeler was less than twenty yards away, directly in the path of the *Queen*. The name painted below the windows of her wheelhouse was *Mississippi Star*. Three men could be seen through the open windows; one struggling with the wheel, another shouting down the speaking tube and the third blasting at the *Queen* with a revolver.

Then the one at the wheel died, as the report of the Mexican's rifle cracked against the eardrums of the group beside the *Queen*'s smokestack.

"Fine shot, señor," Felicity Engle complimented.

Sanchez remained firmly balanced on the trembling deck as he lowered the Winchester from his shoulder, pumped the action, and touched the brim of his black hat.

The helmsman of the *Star* was no longer in sight. The only trace of his former existence was a splash of blood from his shattered head running down the glass panes behind where he had been standing.

The other two men in the sidewheeler's wheelhouse lunged to get the helm as the Mexican's deadly shot signalled an end to the gunfire.

A collision was inevitable now: always had been since Cliff Engle decided to ram the *Star*. But only he had known what was in his mind. Or perhaps the gleaming-eyed woman tightly gripping a handrail had known. Moran and Campbell, too, maybe: one piling cordwood on to the boiler fire, the other sweating to nurse every last ounce of power from the engines. Outwardly at a fever pitch of excitement or exertion—inside as calm as the Mississippi beyond the final surface ripples beyond the influence of the racing paddle-wheels.

Or, if they did not know the precise workings of Engle's mind, they knew the man well enough to trust his judgment in such a situation as this.

Steele, Conners, Burton and Sanchez were fortunate to be with Felicity Engle.

The *Mississippi Star* veered sharply to left and then right, out of control for stretched seconds as the two men in the wheelhouse struggled to get her rudders amidships. The wavering course slowed her. The open water between the surging bow of the *Queen* and the exposed port side of the *Star* inexorably narrowed. To fifteen yards, ten yards, five yards. The water between the two craft was a broiling area of white foam with misty spray above.

The four men beside the smokestack became as resigned to the inevitable as the woman. They gripped the companionway handrail and braced their feet firmly to the deck. Afraid, because they were not fools, but feeling no threat of panic.

Below them, the other gunmen raced aft, abandoning their firing positions on the bow. All except Duke Fargo, who was sprawled face down on the deck under the starboard derrick spar. Some of the men who retreated left gory bootmarks on the deck after stepping into the great pool of blood spilled by the hole in Fargo's belly.

Curses ripped from constricted throats, many of the obscenities linked to Engle's name. There was terror and anger, sometimes a combination of the two, in the voices cutting through the cacophony of sounds made by the racing riverboats.

Then the bow of the *Queen* smashed into the side of the *Star*, just forward of her port paddlewheel.

The momentum of both craft was instantly halted. But nothing was still. The shock of the impact was transmitted to every part of both boats and thence to the water on which they floated.

Only men of great strength were able to retain their handholds as their feet were ripped out from under them. Those who could not hold on, or who had failed to take the precaution, were flung bodily across the decks, sprawling out full length or crashing into bulkheads. Cries of pain were added to the shrieking curses.

It was the same on both boats, but the effects of the collision were felt harder on the sidewheeler. For as her hull was caved in, her timber splitting and her metalwork bending and snapping, she was tilted into a steep list to starboard. Men and equipment were sent sliding across her decks. Her engines stopped and her paddles ceased to turn.

An order was yelled down the speaking tube between the *Queen*'s wheelhouse and engineroom. For little more than a second the big sternwheel was stationary. Then it turned again, the paddles beating the water in the opposite direction. For that second the two boats had been locked together in a clumsy T-shape. Then the *Queen* tore free, dragging her battered bow away from the gaping hole in the side of the *Star*'s hull. The sound of the disengagement was almost as loud as that of the collision had been. The sidewheeler's list was corrected and she floated in a serene drift for a few moments. But a section of the hole was below the water line. And, as the Mississippi torrented into her holds, she tilted in the opposite direction.

Five, ten, fifteen. The yards of open water between the *Queen* going hard astern and the crippled *Star* increased. The sidewheeler's whistle had been silenced several moments before the collision. Now the triumphant Cliff Engle yanked down on a cord in his wheelhouse and held the valve open. The shrill call of high-pressure steam escaping a vent was piercing enough to be painful to some ears.

Then this sound was counterpointed by the deep-throated cheers of men sharing in the triumph of Engle. After being skittled backwards by the momentum of their retreat and the impact of the crash, they now ran forward, eager to enjoy the sight of the enemy in defeat.

On the hurricane deck, Felicity Engle and Conners scrambled to their feet and ran to the forward rail. Below them, the main deck was already crowded at the bow with white men and Negroes struggling to get an uninterrupted view.

But Engle had not yet finished his counter-attack. He swung the rudders hard over and the *Queen*'s juddering took on a new sensation as her hull arced sideways through the water.

Burton had gone down hard and was grimacing the pain of an injured ankle as he hauled himself upright with the aid of the deck rail.

"What does that madman have in mind now?" he growled.

Steele had been forced to release his grip, but a curled arm of the Mexican had prevented him from being flung along the companionway. He nodded his thanks to Sanchez and received a hard-eyed smile for a response.

"His wife said he knows what he's doing," the Virginian answered. And was able to lower his voice to a conversational level for the final word.

For Engle had released his grip on the whistle pull. And after the din of the collision the note of the *Queen*'s engines seemed like a subdued rumble. Punctuated by the shouts and splashes of men leaping off the listing decks of the *Mississippi Star*.

"You believe her?" Burton asked, his tone incredulous as his expression remained pained.

"He had an answer for their mortar," Steele reminded.

Sanchez nodded as the engine noise became even more muted.

The drive had been disconnected from the paddle and the big wheel now turned only because of the river current against it. Engle had maneuvered his craft so that she was headed downriver, in the same direction as the crippled sidewheeler. Now he began to feed power to the wheel again, in short, low-speed bursts.

Lop-sided heavy in the water, the *Star* drifted sluggishly, her bow down low enough so that her stern was out of the water high enough to reveal her rubber blades.

All her crew who were able to move had abandoned their sinking boat. Those who could swim did so, striking out for the *Queen*. Others splashed in panic at the water. Several spilled blood into the mud-colored river—from bullet wounds or injuries they had received on the impact of the collision. Every man was hopeful of rescue as he struggled to get clear of the doomed sidewheeler and near to the other boat.

Until Engle's intention became obvious. For his constant stopping and starting of the paddlewheel had not been designed to close in on the men so they could be taken out of the water. Instead, he had used the engine and the current to bring the boat completely about. So that, as the *Mississippi Star* sank low enough to push her bow into the silt of the riverbed, the *Queen* was stern on to her. And Engle demanded and got full power in reverse.

Felicity Engle and Conners had already run aft. Clint Burton hobbled after them. Steele and the Mexican went in the opposite direction, down the main stairway and on to the now deserted bow. They passed the corpse of Duke Fargo on either side, not even glancing at the inert gunman. And leaned over the side to look down at the prow—as the death toll of the trip to Twin Creeks mounted.

Three men died spectacularly, in the manner Cliff Engle had intended by bringing about the boat and sending her hard astern. Men who could not swim and who were driven into paralysis by the awe-inspiring sight of the huge paddlewheel bearing down on them. With the ending of their panicked flailing of the water, they sank. But they would not have had time to drown before the drag of the wheel gripped them. To suck them up through the bubbling water, which changed colour from white to crimson as the paddles smashed flesh to pulp.

Screams cut shrilly above the throb of the engines and the thrash of timber against water. But not from the men who were caught by the wheel, torn apart, and then had the pieces of their bodies hurled up from the river and catapulted high through the sunlit, spray glinting air. The men with time to vent their terror were those who had escaped the wheel. Who swam through the white wash of the paddle or tried desperately to flail themselves to safety. For whether moving of their own accord or bobbing like corks to the dictates of the water, they were easy targets for the gunmen on the stern of the *Queen*.

Her engines were disengaged again, as Engle gave his men time to finish the killing.

On the boiler deck, Conners and Burton used their handguns, taking careful aim at their targets. Below, the rest of Engle's hired guns were at either side of the wheel. Those who had taken the time to draw rifles from the boots of their saddles used them. Others proved they were as accurate as Conners and Burton with revolvers at short range.

Bullets thudded into flesh and flesh spurted blood. Most of the helpless victims died from head wounds, the men aboard the slowly drifting sternwheeler having the time to take aim at the only visible area of the target.

Men who had swum like experts and others who had fought the river to stay afloat were suddenly buoyant in the inertness of death. Riding the crimson streaked water whole, amid the severed heads and dismembered limbs and torsos of the three who died by the paddlewheel.

"Got metal reinforcement in back of the timber, I

reckon," the Virginian drawled as he straightened up from surveying the bow.

The Mexican nodded.

The prow and the curving hull timbers to either side were splintered and scraped from the ramming action. But they had not caved in.

"You men!"

Steele and Sanchez turned to look up at the wheelhouse as Engle shouted.

"Any damage?" His face was purple tinged with excitement and the bright sunlight gleamed on the sweat bands pebbling his forehead and cheeks.

"Lost some paint is all," Steele reported.

Engle pasted a broad grin across his craggy features. "They lost a whole lot more than that, didn't they?" he yelled, then drowned his own burst of laughter by ordering power to be supplied to the paddlewheel.

The *Queen of the River* had been drifting broadside on down the Mississippi at the insistence of currents. Now, with white foam trailing out behind her, she came about and began to nose northwards again. On the bank astern of the riverboat, Hank and his surviving son were snapped out of the state of horror in which they had watched the slaughter. They began to round up the horses to transport themselves and the dead back to Bradstock Landing.

Horror continued to be inscribed upon many faces aboard the sternwheeler as she steamed past the wrecked *Mississippi Star* and the human flotsam which humped the water alongside her canted hull. Black faces. The faces of men hired to build a railroad: previously unaware of the strength of the opposition to them, and the lengths to which Engle would go to deal with it.

On the faces of the white men—and one woman—

along the port side of the boat there was either triumph or satisfaction as their eyes drank in the sight of death and destruction.

Then the *Queen* rounded the curve of the river and was among the trees where the *Star* had waited in ambush. And what was left of the sidewheeler and her crew were obscured by the thick timber.

The shade of the foliage provided coolness to dry the sweat of excitement and exertion. The engines took up an easy, regular beat, the steam pistons pumping smoothly and the wheel turning almost lazily. It was as if time had slowed down amid the peace and tranquillity of the river swinging this way and that through the timber. Men experienced weariness and hunger. Some felt the pain of minor injuries, suffered a few minutes before, which had been numbed while the danger of greater harm had existed.

Steele was suffering the irritating ache of a torn muscle in his upper left arm. He also felt tired from the loss of four hours sleep while he was on watch during the night. But his main concern was the dirt and sweat and bristles of more than twenty-four hours.

Six blacks were at work in the galley when he entered. They had already set pans of fresh water to boil and skillets of more fat to fry so that coffee could be made and breakfast cooked. Now they were cleaning up the mess of the first attempt: and there was a quality of fearfulness in the manner in which they avoided looking at the Virginian.

"You fellers mind if I take some of this hot water?" he asked as he picked up a tin jug and moved to the line of four stoves.

The men continued to mop the floor and restack the pots and pans.

"I asked," Steele said, pouring steaming water from a pan into the jug. "That makes it all right for me."

80

Still there was no response. But, as he went through the door on to the companionway he sensed their fear-filled eyes looking at him. When he glanced across the after section of the main deck several of the Negroes grouped there were not quick enough in averting their eyes. And he saw the fear in their ebony faces. Some did not look at him at all, as they stared out at the tree lined banks, nursed their own cuts and bruises or attended to the injuries of their neighbors. A few gazed at Steele blatantly. Without fear. Instead, a range of expressions running from despondency to contempt.

"Ungrateful lot of black bastards, ain't they, buddy?" Andy Clapham snarled from his watch station at the starboard stern rail. "We save their stinkin' hides for 'em and all they can do is look at us like we're piles of buffalo chips."

"Just so long as Engle shows his gratitude," Steele drawled. "Fifty times a day."

The bearded Clapham spat over the side. "Like buffalo crap!" he growled. Then, as something splashed over the side at the bow: "What was that!"

He pumped the action of his Winchester. The Negroes became as tense as the gunman and fear seemed suddenly to have a palpable presence in the fetid atmosphere flowing over the closely packed deck. Steele glanced forward and saw Ned McCall standing stoop-shouldered at the bow rail, a morose expression on his bullet-scarred face as he stared down at the river.

Clapham relaxed as the corpse of Duke Fargo slid serenely by, then was caught in the wash from the turning paddlewheel and sucked below the turbulent surface.

"Easy, fellers," Steele told the nervous Negroes. "Just one of the chips going down."

CHAPTER SIX

The Virginian shared a four berth portside cabin with Conners, Burton and Sanchez. Only the Mexican was there when Steele entered. He was stretched out on the straw-filled mattress on one of the cots, fully dressed except for his hat. His right hand tightened around the frame of his rifle which lay alongside his leg, and his eyelids snapped up when he heard the door open. Then he relaxed and closed his eyes again, without altering a line of his unruffled expression.

The cabin was spartan, with no covering on the deck-board floor and no decorations on the bulkheads. There was just one window. In addition to the four cots—and, like them, bolted to the floor—there was a bureau with the mirror long gone from its frame. A tin basin was screwed to the top of the dresser and water leaked out around the screw. So Steele had to strip to the waist and wash and shave fast to beat the leakage. He used a cake of soap and razor taken from his saddlebags, on the heap of gear he had brought to the cabin before going for hot water.

When he had dressed again and dusted off his clothes he still did not feel as clean as he liked to be. But, after an early life when he had been able to have anything he desired, he had learned to make compromises to the dictates of any given situation. And having made the most painful concession of all to his ruling fate, the rest were easy to endure.

His home and his very birthright were gone forever. That had been the hardest reality to face and he had been made to suffer badly in learning this lesson. Many times after the death of his father and Deputy Jim Bishop he had sought to re-establish some semblance of what he had lost. Not in Virginia, for he had known at the moment he was strangling Bishop that he could never return there. But America was a big country and there were many corners of it which offered the opportunity for a man to enjoy a rich and peaceful life. Provided he had the money to pay for more than the basic essentials of living.

But money in any consequential amount always either eluded Adam Steele or was snatched away from him. Until he was forced to admit to himself that his years of youthful plenty had been a trick of his cruel fate: that he had been allowed to enjoy them so that the present and future were bleaker than ever by contrast.

Nowadays, he seldom hankered for what once had been. Not since he had drunk himself free of the need for hard liquor in a tiny Mexican village had he indulged in self-pity for his present lot. Lately, he had abandoned all specific plans for the future. But some old habits and firmly established standards could not be shed. Thus he continued to enjoy the luxuries and finer things of life whenever there was the opportunity. And cleanliness was undoubtedly a luxury in the kind of life he now led.

He was sitting on the side of his cot, reloading the Colt Hartford, when Marv Conners came into the cabin. Sanchez gripped his rifle tighter, but did not open his eyes this time.

"Grub in fifteen minutes," the Texan announced, the

83

familiar grin back on his craggy face. "Ar. plenty of it for them that want it, I guess. Ain't but a handful of them niggers look like they'll be ready to eat until tomorrow."

He lay down on his own bunk, crossing his ankles and interlacing his fingers behind his neck. He let out a long sigh of contentment as he enjoyed the first moments of horizontal relaxation.

"You're hungry, though?" Steele asked.

The tone of voice changed the Texan's mood. To anger. But then he snapped his head around and saw there was no hostility in Steele's expression. And he lay his head back and stared hard at the ceiling.

"Okay, I had the crap scared outta me back at the landin'. And there ain't no reason why you shouldn't know why that happened. I'm rusty as hell. Time was I was trouble shootin' every day of the week for any man who could raise the ante to pay me. Doin' it good and never a worry. But I been up in Wyomin' for best part of five years. Had a wife at the start and four kids as well at the end of it when I quit."

"Farming?" Steele asked.

"Raisin' cattle," Conners replied with a grimace. "And hatin' every lousy minute of it. And believe me, livin' through the best part of five years not likin' it ain't no fun."

"Your family still on your place?"

"I wouldn't know, Steele. They were there in their beds the mornin' I rode out. I guess they are. Had enough stock to provide for themselves. And some good hands to do the heavy work."

"Like killing the beef?"

Conners let out another sigh, this time of resignation. "Yeah, you're right. Killin' ain't hard for a man like me. Men or stock, it's all the same. Exceptin' that men got what it takes to put up an argument with you."

"How long did you spend checking on the competition, feller?"

"Most of a year. Around San Antonio, Laredo, Austin, Houston, Dallas—places like that. And I found out enough to figure I could make it against most of 'em. But then that city kid showed me how slow I'd gotten to be. And I was still scared of knowin' about that when them two teamsters tried to cut the boat free. But I learned from it. All I gotta do is stay outta one for one showdowns. That fight awhile back, that's more my style—and speed."

The grin was back on his face and, just for a moment, the Virginian envied Marv Conners. A man who had made a mistake, taken a clear-cut decision to change course, adapted to a new situation and knew his intentions. But then, as the breakfast call rang out, Steele shook his head in self anger. He had tried that route and failed time and again. Only to discover that grief of one kind or another lay in wait. So to envy Conners was merely to be jealous of his ignorance of the disappointments to come.

As he stood up, canting the Colt Hartford to his shoulder, he saw that Ricardo Sanchez was awake and looking at him with a knowing glint in his dark eyes. And it was as if the Mexican had read Steele's mind from the expression on his face.

"You and me both, feller?" the Virginian tried.

And received a nod of acknowledgement.

Then all three of them went down to the galley: and what Conners had said about the Negroes was proved to be correct. A half dozen were already eating on deck and a few more were in the line waiting to be served. Goldsmith, McCall and Krantz were also on the companionway outside the galley. The Clapham brothers, Frank Potter and Clint Burton were still on watch as the *Queen of the River* thrashed clear of the timber and headed up the calm Mississippi between the shallow slopes of a broad valley.

There was pastureland on the western slopes, being grazed by some fine looking horses. On the eastern shore there was a large cotton plantation with the big house on a knoll in the far distance. Even through the heat haze it was possible to see that little had been done to repair the war damage to the mansion.

Negroes were working the cotton fields and became the objects of envious gazes by the blacks aboard the sternwheeler.

"That's all you niggers are fit for, boy!" Vic Krantz growled at the black man ahead of him in the chow line. "Pickin' cotton for a roof over your stinkin' heads and a bowl of grits two times a day."

"Yes, sur," the Negro answered without turning his head.

" 'Cepting for some of your women, course," Krantz went on as the line shuffled forward. "Some of your women are real good for white men to screw. Long as a white man makes sure to have his black woman scrubbed down before he touches her."

"Yes, sur," the Negro repeated. He wore no shirt under his dungarees. His muscles were bunched under the skin of his broad shoulders and sweat beads bubbled the leather-textured flesh.

McCall was immediately behind Krantz and the young City Sam Goldsmith was in back of McCall.

"He doesn't really like screwing nigger women, nigger," the skinny youngster put in lightly. "It's just that no white woman will look at him after they learn what he likes to do with them. Why, even the whores in New Orleans won't . . ."

"Hey!" McCall snarled, jerked out of morose pensiveness as Krantz whirled.

And Goldsmith uttered a yell of angry surprise as McCall backed hard into him, a sharp elbow jabbing him in the belly.

Krantz overlaid his rage with a brutal grin of triumph as he saw an opening which had always been denied him in the past. For the hollow-cheeked youngster was still recovering from McCall's involuntary move as Krantz lunged into the attack.

"Shift your ass!" he snarled, gripping McCall's upper arm and flinging him hard against the rail. As he drew back his other hand and then drove it forward.

"We ain't never gonna get no breakfast!" Conners complained as he, Steele and Sanchez dodged to the rail of their own volition. And the Negroes at the head of the line scuttled out of the confines of the companionway to join the others on the open deck.

Goldsmith was helpless by then. Screaming in pain and fear as the whip thong curled viciously around him at elbow level. His arms were trapped tight against his body: and although he had a grip on the butt of his Colt, he was unable to draw it from the holster.

Krantz gave vent to his feelings with a bellow of enraged victory. And took a backward step, jerking on the whip.

Goldsmith was spun around by the uncurling action of the thong. His gun cleared leather, but he was disorientated by the spin. Moments of temporary freedom sent a rush of confidence flooding through him. He was facing the wrong way, his blazing eyes staring past Steele, Sanchez and Conners towards Felicity Engle and Frank Potter who were hurrying along the companionway towards the disturbance. There was a lust to kill in the angular, hollow-cheeked, sweat-sheened face of the youngster. Then confusion, followed by a greater depth of terror as his vision cleared and he realised he had his back to the enemy.

He started to whirl, gun hand moving faster than his body.

The whip cracked against thin air. Then hooked over and curled around the thin wrist of Goldsmith's gun hand. He screamed and Krantz roared. A high and a low pitched sound. Flesh was ripped off the bone and blood spurted. The Colt thudded to the deck.

Krantz jerked on the whip again. Forcing Goldsmith to complete the turn and then wrenching him forward. Goldsmith's derby scaled from his head and his swinging foot kicked the discarded gun. The hat went over the rail and the gun under it.

"Right!" Krantz snarled, and swung up his free arm to thud the clenched hand against his own chest. He judged the angle and direction of the crooked elbow finely. So that the sharp bone smashed hard into the youngster's Adam's apple. "Right!" the broadly built, ruddy-faced, oddly moustached man snarled a second time.

The repeated word could be heard more clearly. For the blow to the throat had curtailed Goldsmith's scream. And the youngster could utter nothing more than a strangled gasp as he fell hard to his knees.

Krantz backed off a step and drew the whip thong away from the wrist with measured slowness.

Goldsmith's rump dropped on to his heels and he raised both hands. He sucked at the blood on his punished wrist and clutched his bruised throat with his good hand. His eyes were tight closed, but tears of agony squeezed out from under the lids to course down his cheeks, mingling with sweat among the bristles of his jutting jaw.

"Right, I'll f—"

Krantz had drawn back the whip again, trailing the thong across the deck to begin another attack. But his victim's inability to either counter or retreat gave the older man time to relish his victory. And he looked up to grin at his white audience in the companionway.

He saw that Steele and Sanchez were watching him with the cold-eyed calculation of specialists surveying another expert. McCall was morose again, still reflecting on the deaths of his two partners. Conners, like Potter and the woman a few yards away, was eager to see the outcome of the one-sided fight.

Moran was a latecomer to the bystanders. He stood with the double-barrelled shotgun slanted across his chest, wearing an expression of grim expectation on his smoke-sooted face.

And Krantz bit back on the obscenity he had been about to hurl at Goldsmith.

"I'll teach you to keep needlin' me, kid!" he corrected. And the presence of the woman and Moran even caused him to moderate his tone.

But he made no allowances with the whip. He swung it in an overarm action, to lay the thong brutally against Goldsmith's right shoulder.

The youngster uttered a strangled roar of agony and threw himself sideways. He rolled on to his belly, then forced himself up on to his knees and his good hand. He started to scamper forward then: very clumsily, with his bleeding wrist trailing uselessly on the deck.

"Right! Right! Crawl, you little creep! But you're crawlin' the wrong way! To me! To me!"

Krantz was also ungainly as he lunged forward, his stiff right leg having to swing far out to the side as he took each step.

Goldsmith was whimpering. Krantz was laughing. As, with cruel playfulness, the older man straddled the younger to get ahead of him: then whirled and used the punishing whip again.

The first lashing blow down the length of Goldsmith's back stopped him. The second forced him flat

89

on to the deck. The third hit exactly the same area as the others—directly along the line of the spine. And Goldsmith became still and silent, except for the rise and fall and ragged sound of laboured breathing.

Krantz, his glowing red face contorted into an ugly mask of unadulterated hatred, drew back his arm for another lash at the unconscious form. Then launched the whip again.

Steele stepped forward, the Colt Hartford arcing down from his shoulder. But his free hand did not come up to curl around the barrel. Instead, it joined the left at the frame. To share in the strain as the whip thong coiled around the barrel.

"What the . . . ?" Krantz snarled, and replaced words with a howl of frustration as a sharp sideways movement of the rifle wrenched the whip handle from his grasp. He half-turned to face the Virginian, his rage and hatred deepening.

Gasps of surprise and growls of disappointment sounded on three sides of the two men. Then there were just the noises of the sternwheeler's progress through the water. As Krantz dropped both hands to fist around the butts of his two revolvers.

The Virginian's gloved thumb pulled back the hammer and the rifle's cylinder clicked around. Krantz stayed his hands on the guns and his glowing eyes dropped their gaze from Steele's face to the barrel of the rifle with the whip still hanging from it.

"Just 'cause he's a dude like you?" the glowering man rasped. "That make you big buddies?"

Steele did not reveal the fear that lurked in the pit of his belly. Nor the contempt he had for Krantz's lack of self-control. Had it not been for his dark eyes, his lean and sun bronzed face would have have been impassive. But the steady gaze of his eyes conveyed to Krantz the

Virginian's readiness to kill if he had to. His tone was conversational.

"Just doing my job, feller. Which is to protect the blacks on this boat."

"Goldsmith ain't no nigger!" Krantz snarled. "So what you buttin' in for? This is personal!"

"So settle it on your own time," Steele answered. "Which will be after we get the blacks to Twin Creeks."

Krantz narrowed his eyes, tightened his mouthline and creased his forehead. Everyone who could see his face knew they were watching a man struggling to produce a clear thought from a mind in turmoil. Then the fat lips curled back to display stained teeth in a sneer.

"Engle payin' you over the odds to keep the rest of us in line?" he taunted, looking to left and right in search of support for the idea.

Steele continued to watch Krantz's face and saw from the rekindling of anger visible in it that nobody was prepared to take sides.

"I know that ain't true, Steele!" Moran growled. "So what's with you?"

"We started with fourteen guards counting you and the engineer, feller," the Virginian answered evenly. "The opposition has already taken care of two of them. I reckon we can't afford to lose any more unless we have to."

"Sure makes sense," Conners offered.

"That's damn right!" Cliff Engle agreed angrily, elbowing his way between his wife and Moran to stride along the companionway. "What in tarnation is the trouble here?"

"Who's got the wheel, sir?" Moran asked.

"Burton! And he'll keep on doing a good job with it if you give him steam!" He glared briefly at the mean-faced stoker, who turned and hurried back to the boiler, then surveyed Steele and Krantz again. "Well, I asked a question?"

Krantz was the one provoked to answer. He let go of his twin Colts and slapped his stiff leg. "Goldsmith and me got into a fight over a girl once," he rasped. "And I ain't never been able to walk proper like after he winged me in the knee. And all the time we're around each other, he needles me." He glared down at the inert Goldsmith with a vicious grin. "The little snotnose had it comin' to him."

Engle nodded his satisfaction with the explanation. Then stepped in front of the levelled Colt Hartford and uncurled the whip thong. There was an expression akin to relief in his pale blue eyes as they fleetingly met the uncommunicative gaze of Steele. Then he put his back to the Virginian and thrust the whip into the hands of the startled Krantz.

"Very well. You have now punished the man who incapacitated you. I would warn you to leave it there. I will tell the same thing to Goldsmith when he is in a fit state to listen."

He glowered at Krantz and had to wait a full three seconds before he received the response of a reluctant nod. Then he snapped his head around to look towards the Negroes and stabbed a finger at two of them. "You and you! Pick up the injured man and bring him to his cabin. Whoever shares with him will take care of his injuries." Now he looked at Steele and Sanchez in a single short glance before pulling his shoulders back and striding along the companionway. "You two men will come to my cabin just as soon as you've eaten."

He gripped the upper arm of his wife with enough force to bring a cry of pain from her lips. And she could do nothing except turn and take running steps to keep up with him across the forward main deck and up the stairway.

"You'd have blasted me to save that punk?" Krantz rasped at Steele as the two designated blacks moved tentatively to roll Goldsmith on to his back and lift him clear of the deck. "Still have made a man short, dude!"

"You got lucky, feller," the Virginian answered, uncocking the rifle and sloping it to his left shoulder before coming away from the rail to head for the galley doorway. "Fast gun just has to be better than a feller with a whip in the kind of trouble we have. Unless your luck holds."

"Shit on that! Luck didn't have nothin' to do with it! I beat that snotnose sonofabitch fair and square! And what you think these are, dude? Decoration?"

Steele halted on the threshold of the galley to look back at Vic Krantz. The man had thrust the bunched-up bullwhip into his pants waistband and fisted both hands around the twin Colts in their holsters.

"Reckoned they were ballast, feller," the Virginian replied evenly. "Hold you down when you get all filled up with hot air."

Krantz teetered on the edge of violent action again, but controlled himself. "You got a smart mouth, dude," he growled after stretched seconds of tense silence. "The kind that just asks to be closed for good every time it opens."

Steele sighed. "I'll do you a favor, feller."

Krantz blinked. "What?"

"Have breakfast. And it's not polite for a man to eat with his mouth open."

CHAPTER SEVEN

Cliff Engle had not arranged any special privileges for himself on the trip from Bradstock Landing to Twin Creeks. His three berth cabin at the forward end of the starboard companionway was as spartanly furnished as those of his hired gunmen. The sea chests which showed under the other two cots indicated that he was sharing with Moran and Campbell. But the two crewmen were absent on duty when Steele and Sanchez entered.

Engle was sitting on his own cot, back against a bulkhead and arms hugging his folded legs. The Clapham brothers were lounging on one of the other cots, Andy cleaning his Winchester with an oiled rag while his elder brother absently finger-combed his beard.

Engle had undressed to suit pants, hose and undershirt. He was unshaven and sweat-run and weary-eyed. The Claphams were still fully dressed in their Western garb, complete with Stetsons. Their mood was a mixture of impatience and boredom.

"Awful nice of you boys to show up," Stan growled.

"Enough of that!" Engle snapped, apparently jerked out of a period of deep thought by the entrance of the two newcomers. "That kind of attitude is the very reason I asked you men here to straighten out."

Stan shrugged and Andy rested his gleaming rifle across his thighs. Steele and Sanchez leaned against the bulkheads either side of the door.

Engle gave a curt nod of satisfaction as the silence lengthened. Then sighed and blinked several times. He continued to look close to exhaustion.

"Fine. First I have to apologise to you men. For not taking you into my confidence from the outset. But, to be frank, I had not realised my methods of recruitment would produce men of your calibre."

"Just figured to get point forty-five Colts and Winchesters, uh Mr. Engle?" Stan Clapham suggested with a humourless grin.

"With dumb clucks to squeeze the triggers?" Andy added.

He howled as his brother rapped him hard on the ankle with a boot heel. Then Stan injected some warmth into his grin as he looked across the cabin at Sanchez. "My kid brother didn't mean nothin' personal, buddy."

The Mexican shook his head and parted his lips. His dark eyes indicated he was prepared to reserve judgement.

"When I gave my agents their assignments, I specified the kind of men I wanted for this trip. And I got some of precisely that kind. Krantz and Goldsmith. Potter and Conners. McCall and the one who was shot." He clicked a thumb against a finger in the humid air of the cabin, genuinely failing to recall the name of a man now dead and therefore of no further use to him.

"Willard Breen," Andy Clapham offered.

"Breen was more than a trigger finger," Steele put in. "He means Fargo."

Engle made the clicking sound again, and pointed one of his fingers at the Virginian. "Yes, Fargo."

"You missed out the man from Boston," Stan said.

Engle shook his head. "I place Burton in the same group as you men. But he is already proving useful as a relief for me at the helm."

"If he wasn't, you'd just drink lots of coffee?" Stan wanted to know.

Engle sighed. "I'm not conducting this interview very well, am I?" he asked himself. Then cleared his throat. "I was master of a Union blockade vessel during the war. Wyatt Moran was my first officer. Russ Campbell has been around riverboats all his life. We can all handle the *Queen* from the wheelhouse. And anyone—black or white—can take care of the boiler and engines if there's no problem."

"But you like Burton better than them two?" the elder Clapham put in when Engle paused for breath.

His brother had lost interest in the talk and was using the oiled rag on the Winchester again.

"I happen to consider that intelligence has a bearing on coolness in a crisis, Mr. Clapham. And there can be no argument that intelligence and initiative are connected."

He shot a distasteful glance at Andy, and was surprised in the act by a look from Stan. For a moment, Engle was anxious. Then he relaxed when the elder brother was not provoked to anger.

"Andy?"

"Yeah, Stan?"

"Beat it."

"Sure, Stan."

He rose and went out of the cabin, grinning his appreciation of his opportunity to do so. While the door was open, a pleasant river breeze wafted in, cooling sweat and neutralising the smells of unwashed bodies. But the bad odors soon built up again after the door was closed.

"I ain't never been a man to deny the truth, buddy," Stan Clapham told Engle levelly. "Andy ain't so bright."

"I thought, seeing as how you are brothers . . . "

"Nice you thought that way."

Engle cleared his throat again, to end the lengthening silence. "Fine. I intend that to be the last mistake I make on this trip."

"You've done all right so far, buddy."

Engle waved away the compliment. "I know about ships and how to handle them. How to fit them out. So the *Queen* has a new boiler and the latest engines to make her faster than she looks."

"And a reinforced front end," Steele reminded.

"Just so." The glance he directed towards the Virginian suggested he still did not quite believe what he was seeing. "I tried to foresee every eventuality and to make preparations for it. But I underestimated the size, strength and variety of my opposition. And its determination. First those two teamsters—misguided innocents that they were. Then the men from the landing, in the pay of or perhaps merely influenced by a Garrett man. Their attempt to stop us obviously planned in close conjunction with the riverboat attack."

"Harder than you figured it'd be, uh?"

Engle swung his legs over the side of the cot and straightened his shoulders. Grim determination supplanted weariness on his face. "But nothing that can't be handled now I've adjusted to it." His tone of voice was as grim as the expression on his ruddy face. Then he became almost pathetically pleading in his attitude as he added: "Providing you men are willing to go along with my plan? Which will place additional responsibilities on you. Of course, you will be rewarded with extra pay."

"We're listenin', buddy," Clapham said into the pause as Engle waited expectantly.

He received an impassive nod from the Mexican.

"Mr. Steele?"

"Listening and counting, feller. I'll tell you what number I've reached after I've heard you out."

It was ninety minutes later when Cliff Engle appeared on the forward edge of the wheelhouse deck and surveyed the closely packed group of white men and Negroes assembled below him. It had taken him only a third of that time to get what he wanted from Steele, Sanchez and Clapham—at the price of double pay. Then he had gone back to the aft main deck to talk with the acknowledged top man of the Negroes.

Now, with the exception of the injured Goldsmith in his cabin, Clint Burton in the wheelhouse, Felicity Engle standing watch on the stern and Moran and Campbell tending the boiler and engines, the stoutly-built, craggy and red-faced Engle commanded the attention of everyone aboard the *Queen of the River*.

"Fine, you men!" he shouted. "Now listen and listen good. To ensure the safety of this ship and all aboard her, it's been necessary to establish a chain of command. By the very nature of your line of business, some of you won't like it. But it's the way it has to be. And if you feel strongly enough about it, you'll be free to leave the ship at our first refuelling stop."

Sitting on the angle of the rail at the forward port corner of the hurricane deck, Steele watched the reactions of the hired guns. And saw that Andy Clapham had already been made aware of the situation by his brother. For Andy was not even listening to Engle as he leaned on the rail and gazed out at the passing scene on the east bank. A monotonous vista of flat grassland, featured here and there with clumps of timber and on occasional small farm.

Potter and Krantz, McCall and Conners were deeply interested: already disgruntled by the knowledge that there had been a conference without their presence.

And they kept switching their aggrieved attention between Engle, Steele, Sanchez and Stan Clapham.

"I'm in charge of the operation of the ship. With Mr. Burton as my deputy. Likewise, Mr. Moran and Mr. Campbell will command their particular provinces. They will be assisted and relieved by some of you islanders to be designated by your head man."

Ever since the attack by the *Mississippi Star*, the underlying mood of the Negroes had been fearful. Now there was a lessening of tension on shiny black faces. They were still apprehensive about what lay ahead on the sun-glinting broadness of the river, but at least the white man on the upper deck was not demanding more of them than they were prepared to give.

The gunmen who had not taken part in the discussion with Engle remained taut with expectancy. So far they had heard nothing to quarrel with. But now . . .

"Mr. Conners and Mr. Krantz. Your watch and battle stations will be the upper decks. And you will take your orders from Mr. Steele."

The Texan and the man with the bullwhip in his belt both whirled to glare at the Virginian squatting casually on the rail. Krantz stoked his rage. Conners adjusted his mood to one of tacit challenge.

Engle hurried on. "Mr. McCall and Mr. Goldsmith—when he has recovered—will be under the command of Mr. Sanchez on the forward main deck."

"And just how the hell are me and the dude kid supposed to know what the Mexican wants us to do?" Ned McCall called. Not angrily. His expression and tone were sour as he raised the reasonable point.

"You have eyes and he has hands, man!"

McCall simply nodded, and glanced unenthusiastically at Sanchez who was standing at the head of the stairway.

The Virginian pursed his lips and nodded to himself,

realising that the man with the bullet-scarred face was probably happy to be part of a trio again after losing whatever comfort he drew from the partnership with Breen and Fargo.

"The elder Mr. Clapham will command the after main deck. His brother and Mr. Potter will take their orders from him."

"Damn it, I've worked riverboats!" the one-eared Potter complained. "It oughta be me runnin' the wheelhouse with you instead of that smooth-talking Boston guy!"

"When d'you ever steer a sternwheeler from the gamblin' saloon, buddy?" Stan Clapham countered.

"That ain't the point! How come that Burton guy gets to . . . "

"Mr. Engle figures he has a natural talent for it! Same way you got a natural talent for gettin' beat up, buddy. By the looks of you, anyway."

Potter figured the place where his left ear had once been. Then ran a hand over the cuts and bruises he had received in the trouble with Sanchez. His forehead furrowed as he struggled to find a retort.

"That's it!" Engle concluded. "The choice is yours. Agree to this, or leave the boat at Tucker's Ferry."

He swung around to go to the wheelhouse. The Negroes waited for a gesture from their head man, then trailed him down the stairway. Vic Krantz fingered the handle of his whip and waited until there were just white men on the hurricane deck.

Then he snarled: "You guys and him'd be in a real fine mess if the rest of us got off at Tucker's Ferry." He shared his scornful stare between Steele, Sanchez and the elder Clapham. And jerked a thumb over his shoulder towards the spot on the upper deck vacated by Engle. "On account of how you'd be sure to be out-gunned the next time you're hit."

"Maybe, buddy," Clapham answered easily. "But we wouldn't have to keep lookin' over our shoulders at the men supposed to be on our side.

Krantz spat forcefully at the deck. "You know ain't no man gotta do that around me, Stan. I'm not a back-shooter. But I'm hired to guard the stinkin' niggers! And next time the crap starts to fly I'll do just that. My way!"

He bunched a fist and then stabbed out the index finger towards Steele, without looking at the Virginian.

"Do that, feller," came the soft-spoken response.

"Aim to!"

"Unless I give you a specific order," Steele continued in the same even tone.

"You'll do what, punk?"

"Blow out your brains, feller."

Now Krantz showed his sneering face to the Virginian. "From behind, maybe you'll have a chance!" he taunted.

Steele eased off the rail and headed for the stairway, passing close to where the broad-shouldered, short-necked man stood, feet apart and both hands hovering close to the butts of his matched Colts.

"How else would I put a bullet up your ass?" the Virginian asked softly.

Stan Clapham vented a harsh roar of laughter. Everyone else grinned. Then, abruptly, the humor was curtailed.

Sanchez made to level his rifle. The elder Clapham reached for his holstered gun. Two members of a group intent upon protecting a third. The other watchers were simply eager to see the outcome of new violence.

Steele appeared totally unaware of danger. His attitude was of nonchalant relaxation and his face revealed only the fact of his tiredness. But, an instant later, the transformation was complete. In the blinking of an eye, he had opened his left hand and brought his right up to the side of his neck. And turned from the waist before the stockplate of the Colt Hartford hit the deck. His right hand was still moving, coming away from the neck now—fisted around one weighted corner of the sweat-stained kerchief.

The youthful quality that attached to his features in repose was suddenly gone. His thin lips were slightly curled back to show the whiteness of his teeth. His eyes had narrowed a fraction, their blackness abruptly gleaming with an inner fire. The sun bronzed skin had a new kind of sheen as it was stretched taut over the bones.

And it was apparent that his lean body beneath the stylishly cut clothing had also undergone a fast change from casual looseness to rock hard tension.

Steele did not accept Krantz's boast that he would not shoot a man in the back. But had guessed he would not do it in front of an audience. And, as he turned to see Krantz he was proved correct.

The man had lost precious time in snatching a hand away from the gun in the holster to grasp the whip. Surprise at Steele's fast movement slowed him still further.

And the thong of the whip was still unfurling when the silk of the thuggee scarf curled around the side and back of his neck.

He grunted his confusion and swung back his arm. Steele completed his turn and moved his trailing leg forward to step up close to Krantz, bringing his left hand up under his right arm. The free, weighted corner of the scarf arced around the other side of Krantz's neck and was captured in Steele's left hand.

Krantz's hand holding the whip went out to the side and started forward. Steele tucked one elbow into the crook of the other one and wrenched his hands to the side. Right to left and vice versa. Krantz gaped his mouth wide to suck in lungsful of hot, late-morning air. And uttered a choked shriek of panic as his windpipe was constricted: trapping old breath inside him and admitting no fresh. Then his eyes bulged and his face shaded from red to purple as he experienced the agony of the silk cutting into the flesh of his neck.

He dropped the whip and raised both hands, fingers clawed, to try to tear the strangling scarf away from his throat. But there was no gap for his fingers to gain a grip.

For a moment, he attempted to switch from defence to attack, pushing his clawed hands forward in an effort to dig his nails into the sparse flesh of Steele's face.

The Virginian leaned his head back, tightened the scarf another fraction of an inch and jerked his hands downwards.

Krantz flapped his mouth, but only the merest of sounds emerged from his spittle-run lips. Yellow slime oozed from his flared nostrils. His kneecaps rapped hard and painful on the deck as Steele's move forced him into a kneeling posture.

"You'll kill him, buddy," Stan Clapham warned without concern.

Steele ignored him. The river rippled against the hull of the boat. The paddlewheel turned. Smoke billowed from the twin stacks. A flock of starlings glided across the face of the sun. The engines throbbed. A Negro voice, bass deep, began to sing a sad spiritual.

Krantz's mouth ceased to flap and hung open like that of a dead man. The lids began to close over the eyes. His complexion attained the color of a fresh cut beetroot. His rump settled on to the backs of his legs and his hands lay limply on the deck, palms upwards.

The Virginian sighed and opened his left hand. He stepped back, drawing the scarf from around the man's neck and swinging it up over his own shoulder.

Krantz snorted in a great breath of air and toppled on to his side. Steele stooped, retrieved the Colt Hartford and canted it to his left shoulder. Krantz began to pant, then started a racking cough as his air-starved lungs were satiated.

A long shadow was abruptly thrown across the deck, and all except the suffering Krantz looked up towards Cliff Engle.

"Why aren't you men at your stations?" he demanded. Then he saw Krantz, gasping for breath and kneading the flesh of his throat. "Goddamnit, not more trouble!"

"Sure didn't look like it caused Steele none, buddy," Stan Clapham answered, failing to hide all traces of his admiration.

"Mr. Krantz seems to be in a bad way!"

"Just a pain in the neck is all, Mr. Engle," Marv Conners replied, and spat over the rail.

"Which might just keep him from being a pain in the ass," Steele added.

CHAPTER EIGHT

The *Queen of the River* ploughed her way relentlessly up the Mississippi, her engines throbbing at full ahead except on the tightest and narrowest curves.

Shouts of anger and fear were hurled after her whenever she closed with smaller craft, by men who had to fight the turbulent water of the sternwheeler's wake to keep afloat.

The officers, crew and passengers of larger boats were often just as incensed or enraged by the speed and course of the *Queen*. For neither Engle nor Burton made any allowance for other stern- or sidewheelers, whether headed up or down river.

With steam siren shrieking, the man in the wheelhouse held his helm firmly amidships and it was other craft which had to alter course, veering sharply to left or right to leave open water for the racing *Queen*.

Only after the danger of collision had passed did the experienced eyes of rivermen look hard at the retreating sternwheeler and express curiosity about such a decrepit looking boat having so much power.

Others, more concerned about the *Queen's* handling than her appearance, took note of the apprehensive Negroes and the grim-faced white men on her decks. The former as fearful of the present danger as anybody aboard the passing craft; the latter with rifles in their

105

hands and unblinking eyes which searched for the first sign of a different kind of threat.

Even when there were no other boats in sight and the sternwheeler was trailing white water between banks which offered no cover for ambushers, tension remained an unwelcome passenger aboard the *Queen*. A brand of tension compounded from the anxiety of Cliff Engle, the much deeper fear of the Negroes and the resentment between certain of the gunmen.

Two days and two nights slipped into history before the river forked, the broad Mississippi meandering northwards while the narrower Red swung away to the north-west, continuing the diagonal course across the state of Louisiana. The days had been blisteringly hot and the nights humid. Sunbright and softly moonlit.

In all that time the only threats to the *Queen of the River* had been posed by the reckless haste of her progress. And this period of inactivity for all except those engaged in running the boat or feeding those aboard served to build new layers of nerve jangling tension.

With vivid memories of the violence which marked the start of the trip, Engle and the Negroes became increasingly anxious about when the enemy would strike next. While several of the guards began to wonder if they would ever see action again on the journey to Twin Creeks. To such an extent that for long periods, both on and off watch, they ignored the potential dangers from beyond the sternwheeler and made plan after plan about how to deal with their personal enemies on board.

Steele was aware of what was running through the minds of Krantz, Potter and Goldsmith. Each man carried the easy-to-see scars of punishment he had been forced to take from another. The dark bruises around Krantz's neck and the way he limped whenever he walked. The scabs of healing skin breaks on the face of

106

Potter. The ugly wound which the bullwhip had delivered around Goldsmith's right wrist.

It was in the eyes of the men that they betrayed their intention to even these scores. Eyes which were morose in repose, but burning with the low fire of nurtured hatred whenever they fell upon the man or men who had caused their suffering.

But no man made a move against another. And, as more and more miles slipped behind the thrashing sternwheel, the atmosphere of silent hatred thickened to an extent where it seemed to have a taste and a stink.

One daily event kept the explosive situation under control, however. A tour of the sternwheeler each evening after supper by Felicity Engle. It was the only time she emerged from her cabin and the sight of her as a desirable woman among men eager for release from boredom might have served to spark the powder keg of trouble that was the *Queen of the River*. But in the present circumstances the men's lust for money was greater than for a woman. And the knowledge that each night they would receive another bulky package of bills kept the men in line.

Then, as dawn broke on the third day from Bradstock Landing, Clint Burton sounded the steam whistle signal and the prospect of a fuel halt to interrupt the monotony of river travel gave the gunmen a new sense of eagerness in their job.

Those who had been asleep in their cabins emerged on to deck expecting to see precisely what they did. For, as she had handed out the pay envelopes the previous evening, Felicity had told the men that her husband planned to reach Tucker's Ferry in the morning. There had been no need for the woman to add that Engle suspected there would be trouble at the stop. Often during the time when the only reaction by strangers to the sternwheeler had been inactive anger, Cliff Engle had patrolled the boat, urging the guards to stay alert and warning them to beware of anything unusual.

And a break in the headlong progress of the *Queen of the River* was certainly out of the ordinary. Then, as Tucker's Ferry came in sight, men whose line of work made them sensitive to danger signs recognised a menacing atmosphere infiltrated through the hot, damp air.

There was just a single building on the west bank of the river. It was constructed of timber under a pitched roof. The landing stage which ran alongside the bank was long enough to provide mooring for three boats the size of the *Queen*. It was stacked with a large quantity of cord wood, the logs neatly cut to a uniform size. On the other three sides of the building was a large area dotted with the stumps of felled trees. Beyond this was a vast acreage of growing trees. A wheel-rutted trail ran among the stumps between the landing stage and the edge of the forest.

Three empty flatbed wagons were parked to one side of the building. A half dozen horses were in a rope corral to the other side. Smoke spiralled up from a chimney and lamp light gleamed at the three windows visible to the men aboard the approaching sternwheeler.

In the wheelhouse, Burton sounded the whistle again. Not for the benefit of the gunmen, for he knew all would have been roused by the first call. This time it was to ensure that the men who tended the fuel stop and ferry were aware of the presence of the *Queen of the River*.

But the door to the building, which opened directly on to the boarding of the landing stage, remained firmly closed. And nobody silhouetted themselves against the lighted windows.

"Watch all sides!" Engle yelled as he ran up the

stairway to the topmost deck and entered the wheelhouse.

His voice carried to most parts of the boat, for the engine noise and thrash of the paddles against the water was subdued, Burton having ordered a speed of slow ahead as he swung the bows to bring the craft alongside the deserted landing stage. But the order it conveyed was unnecessary.

Steele, the elder Clapham and Ricardo Sanchez had already given a similar command by word or hand signal. For Tucker's Ferry was the perfect place for an ambush, on land or water. The river was only fifty yards wide here and, except for the area of felled timber and a much smaller space where the ferry could dock on the opposite side, trees grew down to the water's edge at both banks. And a hundred yards beyond the ferry, the river veered sharply to the left: much as it had two mornings ago when the *Mississippi Star* had *Star* had launched an attack.

But this place was even better: for the trees grew more thickly, and there was even a grey ground mist to offer additional cover. Thus, a half dozen riverboats could lie in wait around the bend. And a whole army could be concealed within rifle range of the docking sternwheeler.

So narrowed eyes surveyed the river in both directions and peered into the timber on each bank. After the earlier attack, every guard now carried a repeater rifle. Fingers were curled to the triggers, and muzzles swept back and forth.

"Moran!" Engle yelled, coming out of the wheelhouse after assuring himself that the cultured Bostonian was capable of docking the boat.

"Yes, sir!"

"We're not going to get any help! You and some of the blacks'll have to handle the lines!"

"Yes, sir!"

Steele was at the hurricane deck rail on the port side, switching his expressionless gaze between the lighted building and the four stacks of cut logs. He heard Wyatt Moran yelling instructions to reluctant Negroes, peppering the orders with obscenities. Then saw two blacks leap from the side of the boat to the landing stage.

"We can afford to lose a couple of niggers, if we have to!" the red-haired, sweaty-face stoker growled to somebody on the aft main deck. Then he hurled a coil of stout line under the rail. "More than us whites, uh kid?"

The engines were idling as momentum scraped the side of the boat against the landing stage pilings.

"I'm with you," Goldsmith answered.

"You're with Engle!" Steele called down. "And every night you find out how highly he values the blacks!"

"A friggin' company man," Moran snarled. Then raised his voice. "Move your asses, you niggers!"

The stern line and bow line were both over the side now. But the ends of the ropes were trailing free along the landing stage: the frightened blacks who had leapt ashore were paying more attention to the possibility of being shot than to the reality of the boat drifting away from them.

Then glass shattered as the windows of the building were smashed. The lamps went out. The door was flung open.

Rifle fire exploded.

. The engines roared at full power. The paddlewheel spun in reverse and the rudders were held hard over to halt the drift and keep the hull against the pilings. Spray was flung high and the river water was beaten to bubbled whiteness.

Only two bullets were blasted over the superstructure

of the *Queen of the River*, sending the unarmed Negroes aboard and ashore diving for the deck and landing stage with screams of terror.

By that time, the message of the breaking glass and doused lamps was transmitted from the brains of the guards to their hands. And rifle stocks had been thudded to shoulders, then pressure applied to triggers.

"Get the lines!" Steele yelled as he cocked the hammer of the Colt Hartford and squeezed off a second shot.

Conners and Krantz came to the rail on either side of him and blasted bullets at the building. Below them, other gunmen fired from the forward and aft main deck.

The Negroes ashore remained pressed to the planks of the landing stage, hands linked to the tops of their heads and arms pressed to their ears. Unaware that the barrage of gunfire all came from the sternwheeler: the bullets cracking through broken windows and open doorway preventing the men inside from replying.

Elsewhere aboard, other men were shouting, but the bedlam of noise—engines, paddles, gunfire and the creaking of hull against pilings—drowned out mere words.

Then two more figures leapt over the side: firing their Winchesters in mid-air and then again as they steadied themselves after hitting the landing stage.

Sanchez at the bow, looking as unruffled as always. And Andy Clapham at the stern—frightened and burning with rage as he glanced back at his brother.

Covering fire continued to be sprayed from boat to the building. But the rifles of the Mexican and the younger Clapham were silent for stretched seconds—as the two men grasped the snaking ends of the mooring lines and coiled them several times around two stakes which served as bollards.

111

The lines snapped taut and creaked at close to breaking strain before the drive was disengaged and the wheel halted its revolutions. The men providing covering fire continued to spray bullets at the building until Sanchez and Andy Clapham reached the cover of log piles.

Then, without an order being given, the gunfire ceased.

A woman was sobbing and a man was groaning. Both sounds came from inside the building. The engines of the *Queen* were at idle again as the steam of unwanted power hissed angrily from safety valves. The acrid stench of exploded powder was stronger than the smells of steam and woodsmoke and mist dampened timber.

"There's a man in here dyin', you crazy bastards!"

The angry voice came from within the bullet-scarred building. And the second half of what it said was very loud: for the young engineer suddenly shut down his engines and the only other sounds in the grey dawn were the ripple of water between dock and boat and a less strident hiss of escaping steam.

"We've all got problems!" Cliff Engle answered, his voice powerful as he spoke between hands cupped at his mouth. "If all you people come out of there with your hands up, you won't be one of mine anymore."

"To be friggin' killed?"

"Not if you do as you're told."

"We ain't gonna trust you!"

"All right. I just hope for the sake of your souls that you trust in God. Let them have it, you men!"

Once more the dawn was filled with the crackle of rifle fire, counterpointed by the thud of bullets into timber and the smash of shattered glass. For perhaps fifteen seconds the barrage was kept up without respite, Sanchez and Andy Clapham adding their fire power from the cover of the logs.

Out in the open, the two Negroes hugged their heads again. But no one had a chance to get a shot out of the building.

Then a balled up blanket was hurled through the open doorway. It hit the landing stage and spread open. Grey, but its message of surrender was clear enough and the rifle fire came to a faltering end.

"Okay, okay! How many more times! We give up!"

He appeared in the doorway. Short and fat and trembling. With blood from a bullet wound blossoming on his left shoulder. His crinkled, sixty-five-year-old face was almost as red as the blood from the effort he had put into shouting against the barrage of gunfire.

"Toss out the irons, buddy!" Stan Clapham ordered.

"Do like he tells us," the man called over his shoulder.

A half dozen rifles sailed out through the door and windows and thudded against the landing stage.

"Andy, Mex!" Clapham growled. "Go get them guns. Toss 'em in the river."

Sanchez moved out from behind the logs instantly. Andy glanced nervously back towards his brother.

"But, Stan, we . . ."

"Do it, brother!" Stan snarled. "Don't stop to count how many guns we got coverin' the old boy."

Andy raked his gaze along the side of the sternwheeler and his nervousness disappeared beneath a broad grin when he saw the levelled rifles. He scuttled forward to help the Mexican as the two Negroes rose unsteadily to their feet.

"Now get your buddies outside," Clapham ordered.

Steele glanced up at the wheelhouse deck. Engle was standing there, unarmed and grinning, thumbs hooked at the armpits of his vest as he watched the activity on the landing stage.

113

"We ain't careful, Steele, Clapham could take over this operation," Conners muttered.

"He couldn't afford it," the Virginian replied, his expression grimly sad as he watched the people file dejectedly out of the building.

There was a woman, as old and worn as the first man to appear. Another, younger, woman with two small boys of about five or six clinging to her skirts. And three men in their mid-twenties. All were poorly dressed but clean. Dull faced and weary. The mother of the two children had been crying, and the first rays of the rising sun—shafting through the trees on the far bank and burning off the mist—gleamed on the fresh tears coursing down from her red-rimmed eyes.

Five rifles splashed into the river at the bow of the moored boat.

"One gun too many!" Clapham growled. "One more too few. The one that was hit, maybe?"

The eldest man looked at the young mother. She shook her head and the tears were abruptly accompanied by howls of anguish. The children looked mournfully up at her and she dropped into a crouch and hugged them to her.

"Dead," the old man said.

"Mr. Engle?" Clapham called, relinquishing authority.

Steele looked again at the man above him and saw that the grin was still firmly in place as Engle yelled at Moran and Campbell to have the Negroes restock the boat's fuel supplies. Then, as the gangplank was slid down from the main deck to the landing stage and the work started, the Virginian moved along the companionway and went up the stairway aft of the wheelhouse deck.

"You didn't have to kill nobody!" the old man called

dully. "Them shots we fired was just for warnin'! To let you know we didn't want you at our place!"

"I need logs for my boiler!" Engle growled at him.

"Plenty of trees around, mister! Why d'you have to bother decent folks?"

"Hold your tongue!"

"Hey, you sayin' we ain't decent folks?" Krantz snarled.

"Dunno what dirty name there is to call you!" The old man was losing control of his temper. His face, which had become pale, was flushing again. "Runnin' in cheap nigger labor to take work away from white men!"

"Nigger lovin' bastards about says it!" one of the young men supplied, glaring directly at Krantz.

"Why, you . . ."

Krantz failed to find an insult strong enough to top the one hurled at him. And resorted to the Winchester in his hands.

"No more!" the woman shrieked as the rifle swung. And hurled herself to the landing stage, forcing the children to go down with her.

The men and old woman backed away, all terrified by the expression on Krantz's face.

"Krantz!" Engle roared.

The rifle exploded, the sound freezing the Negroes who were toting great weights of logs across the landing stage and up the gangplank on to the boat.

The man who had accused Krantz of being a nigger lover was hit in the heart. At short range, the rifle bullet drilled through his body and emerged at the back to thud into the timber of the building. The man, dead on his feet, was carried backwards for more than a yard by force of impact and spasming muscles. He hit the door-jamb and was thrown full length to the landing stage,

115

face down, to reveal the large, gory mess of the bullet's exit hole.

"Dear God!" the woman screamed, forcing down the heads of her children so they could not see the new corpse.

Clint Burton emerged from the wheelhouse, an expression of revulsion making his good-looking face suddenly ugly. He joined Steele in gazing at Cliff Engle.

They saw anguish in the pale blue eyes as they swung from looking at the dead man, to Krantz, to the two gunmen close to him.

"Murder," he croaked. And put out his arms, the palms of his hands uppermost in a gesture of helplessness. "What do I do?"

Conners solved the problem for him. Many others might have done, but the tall, craggy faced Texan was nearest to the killer.

"Unarmed, you friggin' maniac!" Conners snarled, swinging around and wrenching the Winchester from Krantz's hands.

He dropped his own rifle at the same time as he hurled the other man's across the deck. Then he backtracked fast, right hand poised to draw his holstered Colt.

Steele, Burton and Engle reached the forward edge of the wheelhouse deck. Sanchez took several paces towards the boat before he halted. Clapham and Potter were still running along the portside companionway of the lower deck when Conners yelled:

"Draw!"

Krantz was still boiling at being called a nigger lover. And Conners's actions and words had stoked the anger. With a roar of rage, he drew. Both handguns.

He should have died then, full of hatred and fury against a man who had all the advantages. For Conners was already in the gunfighter's stance: sideways on to

116

his opponent with his feet apart and firmly set. Ten feet away, with his back to the rising sun. Impassively calm as he prepared to put his skill to the test.

Two Colts cracked and two bullets smashed into vulnerable flesh.

Marv Conners stiffened and moved his gaze away from Krantz to look down at the unfired Remington in his right hand. There was a deep sadness in his blue eyes. Then his legs buckled and his knees hit the deck hard.

"Away too long," he rasped as the revolver slipped from his hand.

The other hand still had feeling in it and he raised it to his chest, dragging it across from one side to the other. The action smudged the blood from both bullet holes into a single stain on the front of his fringed shirt. He died then, tipping forward to slam his chest and face against the deck.

"Krantz!" Steele called softly into the shocked silence.

The broadly built man turned only his square face towards the Virginian. The stronger emotions were draining out of him and his discoloured teeth showed under his Mexican-style moustache in a grin of triumph and pride.

"It was a fair fight, punk!" he rasped through the teeth.

"We need him!" Engle muttered hoarsely.

Steele ignored the comment. "So is this, feller," he said to Krantz.

The Colt Hartford was canted to his left shoulder. Krantz still had his matched Colts drawn, but aimed at where they had exploded the killing shots into Conners's body.

Krantz closed his lips into a tight line. Then they

hardly moved as he taunted: "You been askin' for it long enough, punk!"

The hammers of the Colts and the Colt Hartford clicked back in perfect unison. But the rifle slammed down into the waiting palm faster than the revolvers were swung on to target. The naked terror of impending death showed in Krantz's eyes to reveal his knowledge that this was a fight he was doomed to lose.

The Colt Hartford cracked the reality of the pre-knowledge. Krantz died with his eyes wide open, carrying into eternity the expression of fear. He remained ramrod stiff as he fell, and his muscles did not relax forever until he had crashed into the deck.

"Garrett needn't friggin' bother!" Engle snarled. "At this rate we . . ."

"Get them damn logs aboard!" Stan Clapham yelled to curtail Engle's complaint.

"Mr. Engle?" Wyatt Moran called up from the landing stage. He was as angry as Engle and kept opening and closing his big hands, as if trying to will the double-barrelled shotgun into them.

"Do it!" Engle confirmed after a short pause.

"Move your asses, niggers!"

There was no pause this time: the Negroes responded immediately and worked faster than before.

"Time for another talk, Steele?" Stan Clapham suggested, still out of sight down on the forward main deck. "Everyone exceptin' the niggers, I figure?"

"I reckon, feller. Soon as we're on the move."

"You want more money for killing your own?" Engle spat through lips set in the crooked line of a sneer.

"Not me, feller," the Virginian replied evenly as he ejected the spent shells from the rifle and fed fresh rounds into the cylinder's six chambers. He glanced down at the inert, loose-limbed, spread-eagled form of Vic Krantz. "Never mix business with pleasure."

CHAPTER NINE

"Because he friggin' well had to!" Stan Clapham snarled at Felicity Engle. "That bastard Krantz was under his command!"

Tucker's Ferry was sliding out of sight astern of the *Queen of the River* as her thrashing paddlewheel drove her towards full speed and the set of her rudders steered her around the curve among the trees. Even as the elder brother snapped his glaring eyes away from the equally angry woman, the landing stage, with its huddle of three men, two women and two children was lost behind the intervening timber.

The conference was gathered on the topmost deck of the sternwheeler, forward of the wheelhouse, where Clint Burton could both remain at the helm and take part in the discussions. The sun was fully risen above the timber now, making its heat felt. But its light was dimmed by the woodsmoke billowing from the twin stacks and trailing out behind the boat.

Engle was leaning against the front of the wheelhouse, arms akimbo and head bowed. Wyatt Moran, holding the shotgun across the front of his body at an acute angle, was standing next to him. The hired guns were in a loose-knit group, rifles at the ready and alert eyes dividing attention between Engle and the wooded banks of the Red River.

Felicity had been pacing up and down between them and the two men before the wheelhouse.

The only white man who had elected to stay below was the young Campbell. He had made it clear that the only things of importance to him were the engines. He had never moved far from them on the entire trip, even sleeping close to where they thudded and strained against their mountings.

The cause of the elder Clapham's outburst had been a question posed angrily by the woman to Steele.

The bearded man had beaten the Virginian to a reply. Now, before she could respond after she halted and swung to glare at Clapham, Moran growled:

"Didn't you make some rule about there bein' no cussin' in front of the lady, sir?"

Engle raised his chin off his chest and unfolded his arms to drag a hand across his weary face. He sighed. "Rules get changed according to circumstances," he muttered, and treated his wife to a mean look as she snapped her head around to study him. "Anyway, I guess Mrs. Engle had a good idea of what this trip would be like when she insisted on coming along."

"Only one thing I knew!" she snarled. "What I warned Dad about—that you couldn't handle it!"

"Where you been all the time, lady?" Stan Clapham chided. "He ain't wrecked this tub—and that's what his job is. Keepin' her afloat and runnin' good."

"While the men under him kill each other off?"

Now Clapham sighed. "Tell her about it, Steele."

"Conners was a fool," the Virginian answered. "A gunfighter too old and too long out to grass to make a comeback."

Clapham shook his head impatiently. "Plain for us all to see. No, tell her why you blasted Krantz."

He jerked a thumb over his shoulder. Back there,

travelling downriver at the whim of the currents and undertows, were the bodies of Krantz and Conners.

"You already told her, feller," Steele reminded him evenly. "He was under my command and he shot down an unarmed man."

Clapham looked long and hard at the Virginian. So did his brother. And Goldsmith. And Burton, Potter and McCall.

"Just that, Steele?" It was Clint Burton who spoke what all of them were thinking. "Didn't your reputation have anything to do with it?"

"Been a long time since I cared what other folks thought about me."

"He friggin' means it, you know that, Andy?" Clapham croaked.

"Well, it's always been plain to see he ain't like the rest of us, Stan."

"Okay, lady!" Stan announced, turning away from Steele and waving a hand in a gesture of dismissal. "It just happened to be Steele got the drop on that crazy Krantz before any one else. But if it had been one of the rest of us blasted him, it'd been to protect ourselves why we shot him." He shook his head. "Hell, I ain't much with words. The man from Boston'll tell it better."

"Or me," Engle cut in while Burton was still organizing his thoughts. He raked his eyes over the men in the group. "Three things in life are important to men like these, Felicity. Staying alive, making money and keeping their good names."

"Good names!" the woman spat.

"As professional gunmen," he elaborated. "Who abide by the rules of their profession. Once they break those rules—by killing an unarmed man or shooting a man in the back—their reputation is tarnished. And their lives are in dire danger. Because their enemies—and it is an occupational hazard of their profession to

121

make enemies—no longer consider it necessary to abide by the rules. Thus, they lay themselves open to being gunned down like dogs. Is that not how it goes, gentlemen?"

"About it," Stan Clapham agreed.

"And it also works by association, ma'am," Burton added. "This trip has already had a lot of advance advertising from the way things have been going. And there'll be a lot said about it after it's over."

"But won't no one be able to say we let Vic Krantz gun down an unarmed man and get away with it," Ned McCall finished.

"Bullshit!" Felicity sneered.

Her husband sighed. "My apologies, gentlemen. For trying to fool you into thinking a daughter of Cole Meline could ever be a lady."

"At least I've never pretended to be anything I'm not!" she snapped at him.

"I reckon we'd all be grateful if you'd settle your family problems some other time," Steele cut in before Engle could continue the slanging match. "Right now we'd like to know the full story about this trip, Mr. Engle."

"Damn right!" Stan Clapham growled.

Engle had not expended all his anger on his wife. He had plenty in reserve which he injected into a glowering look at the waiting gunmen.

"You took the job and you've been taking my money . . . "

"Meline money!" Felicity corrected.

Her husband ignored her. "And you knew what the job was when we left Bradstock Landing."

"You said it was running the blacks to Texas against professional guns, Mr. Engle," Clint Burton said through the wheelhouse window.

"Didn't say nothin' about us goin' up against the likes

of that bunch back at Tucker's Ferry," Frank Potter augmented.

Engle realised his anger was wasted on the gunmen, who spoke to him and looked at him with a total lack of emotion. He tried to grind the weariness out of his eyes with clenched fists. When he dropped his hands to his sides there was an expression of almost pathetic helplessness on his haggard face.

"What about the wagon drivers?" Felicity challenged the impassive gunmen. "And the men from Bradstock Landing who trailed the boat?"

"They tried to kill us, lady," Sam Goldsmith pointed out.

"Did kill Will Breen," McCall intoned mournfully.

"But that at the ferry awhile back," Stan Clapham said. "That was just a bunch of folks figurin' us for somethin' floatin' upriver outta the New Orleans sewer."

"Isn't that where you came from?" Felicity retorted.

She thought she was safe, standing close to Ricardo Sanchez and with Wyatt Moran's shotgun protecting her.

Several of the gunmen were unable to prevent rage cracking their impassiveness. The Mexican's expression remained unchanged. He merely back-handed the woman across the cheek. With enough force behind the blow to knock her to the deck.

Moran growled like an animal in pain and swung the shotgun at Sanchez. Engle leaned forward and chopped his arm down. His hand curled over the twin barrels of the gun and forced them to aim at the deck.

"Mr. Meline wouldn't have done that, sir," Moran rasped as the woman got to her feet and backed off, tears of pain shining in her eyes and her cheek glowing red from the sting of the blow.

"Mr. Meline doesn't own her any more!" Engle answered dully, fixing his wife with a cold stare. "She's

123

mine. And I think I've just been taught how to take care of what I own."

"You . . . " Felicity began. But the depth of the coldness in his steady gaze trapped the curse in her throat. She covered her face with her hands, whirled, and ràn past the wheelhouse to the stairway at the aft end of the deck. The pounding of her footfalls did not mask the sobs that wracked her body.

"Fine," Engle said, with a curt nod towards Sanchez. Then he pulled his shoulders back and held his head high. He looked taller and stronger and less tired. "You men are involved in a power struggle between two very rich men. On the one hand is Cole Meline who intends to become richer by building the Texas–Kansas Railroad. One the other is Alexander Garrett who already operates freight wagons and a stage line along the route of the proposed railroad."

"*Alexander* Garrett," Stan Clapham muttered, stressing the first name as an indication that he now knew the man he was up against.

Steele was the only gunman not to show he had heard of Garrett.

"That's right, you men," Engle continued. "Both cattle barons. Both old. Both with more money than they could ever spend if they lived to be three hundred. Bitter rivals in everything they do."

"How did Garrett fix the strike, feller?" Steele asked.

"By a method you understand really well, Mr. Steele. Money. The Garrett spread reaches to the town limits of Twin Creeks. But the man's influence reaches far beyond the property markers. On every side of the Big-G range are people who depend upon Garrett for their living. Merchants need the business of him and his men. Those without a trade work for Garrett."

"So how did Meline ever get started with the railroad, buddy?" the elder Clapham asked.

"He was the victim of a confidence trick," Engle answered, slump-shouldered and weary looking again. "Garrett talked a great deal about his opposition to the railroad. Which only made Cole Meline more determined to build it. Then, as soon as the Twin Creeks depot was built, the river was bridged and Meline had tied up over a hundred thousand dollars in equipment and supplies, Garrett showed his muscle, so to speak.

"He paid the men more not to work than Meline was paying them to build the railroad. Meline went higher. But not a single man came back to work."

"Garrett had told them that building a railroad doesn't last forever," the Virginian drawled. "And if they did build it, there would be no work for them on his spread when it was finished?"

"Precisely. He also brought pressure to bear on them through the merchants. So so that Meline money would not buy anything in the stores of Twin Creeks. Or any other town within a day's ride of the railroad."

"I don't see why all that should make any difference to these guys," Wyatt Moran growled.

Engle gave him a scornful glance. "We are committed to working for Cole Meline. These men are not. So they do not have to put their lives on the line because of the childish rivalry between two stupid old men."

"The pay's good, buddy," Stan Clapham said to curtail discussion on that point. "But money ain't everythin' unless you're a Cole Meline or Alex Garrett." He glanced at the Virginian. "Or Adam Steele, maybe."

"I'm not up here for the view, feller."

Clapham nodded and returned his attention to Engle. "The landin' and the ferry are a long ways from Twin Creeks. Garrett muscle don't reach that far."

"But a much stronger influence does, does it not? I refer to prejudice against black skin. Something I warned my father-in-law of. But he was aware of it, of course. And his decision to bring in Negro labor was taken with premeditation . . . "

"Damn two dollar words," Andy Clapham muttered.

"He means Meline meant it," Stan explained evenly.

"To quote him exactly, he said that if Garrett wanted the crap to fly, the crap would fly very high indeed," Engle went on. "Which is an indication of the juvenile and reckless stubbornness of both men. And Garrett has capitalized on the situation just as I warned he would. With the fore-knowledge that Negroes were being imported to build the railroad, it was easy for Garrett to broadcast across the South that blacks were to be used to break a strike by whites.

"A distortion of the truth, but how many Southerners would consider questioning such an assertion?" Another sigh. "So that, gentlemen, is why you will be spat upon by decent people. When you are not being fired upon by men paid to stop you reaching Twin Creeks."

"I think you lost 'em, sir," Moran muttered as he surveyed the unresponsive faces of the gunmen. All of them dirty and unshaven except for Steele who had used the respite of the log loading to wash, scrape the bristles from his jaw and dust off his clothes. "Reckon they don't want their reps dented by . . . "

"In my line of business I never do get to work for no angels," Stan Clapham cut in. "Sometimes get to fightin' 'em. But not now, I figure. Seems to me there ain't nothin' to choose between Garrett and Meline. How say you, buddies?"

He finger-combed his beard as he raked his questioning gaze over the faces of the gunmen.

"I'm with you, Stan," his brother responded.

"Without me, you ain't nothin'."

The younger Clapham did not allow the retort to spoil his easy grin.

Sanchez gave his mute nod.

"Sure," Goldsmith growled.

"Figure to personally make Garrett pay for gettin' Will and Duke killed," McCall said bitterly.

"In too deep to pull out," Frank Potter added.

Burton said: "Always did like to finish what I started."

"Just leaves you, buddy," Stan Clapham said to Steele after he had failed to join the chorus of agreement. "You want in or out of this big money game?"

"Bearing in mind that you are all merely pawns, Mr. Steele," Engle added miserably, apparently dejected that the attitude of the gunmen forced him to continue with the trip.

"And it's black against white," Clint Burton augmented lightly.

The Virginian showed a cold smile. "Reckon I'll stay on board."

CHAPTER TEN

Felicity Engle died badly. In agonizing pain, with journey's end in sight.

After many days—nobody kept count of how many—during which the sternwheeler was allowed unhindered passage up the Red River. Diagonally across Louisiana, a swing through the south-west corner of Arkansas, then almost due west to mark the border between Texas and Indian Territory. For most of the time the country spread out from either bank was devoid of human presence.

When the *Queen* did reach an infrequent settlement she thrashed her way by without halting. No shot was fired at her, but there was an almost palpable emanation from each small community or isolated homestead which slid by on the port or starboard side of the boat, generated by men and women—even children—who interrupted their chores, lessons or active recreations to stand on the banks and stare at the speeding sternwheeler.

And speed she did for most of the way, Moran and his assigned blacks keeping the firebox full and roaring to supply high pressure steam for Campbell's engines. The only danger to her was that she might ground on a sandpit or smash her paddlewheel on a snag. But, whenever there was a sign of such a potential disaster, the experienced Cliff Engle was called to the wheelhouse to handle the helm and the power of the engines with easy skill.

The reduced complement of guards had split into two watches and covered the boat from stem to stern during the day and night. But even the men who patrolled the decks during the hours of darkness were not spared the hostile stares of hatred from the banks. For the noise of pumping engines and the splashing of paddle blades through the water always announced the approach of the *Queen of the River* even if expanses of timber or the humps of high ground hid her from sight until the last moment. And always she was expected, so that even the soundest sleeper was attuned to wake up as she came close.

"Have you seen a telegraph line since you left New Orleans, feller?" Steele asked Sanchez one overcast, moonless night as the sternwheeler thrashed between two small settlements, one on either side of the river in Arkansas.

The Mexican shook his head, then returned his attention to the village on the east bank.

The Virginian was watching the west bank, seeing the flickering lights of lanterns swinging in the gusty wind, held aloft by men and women who were merely dark shadows against yellow cones. Until a lamp was swung at a wider angle to briefly illuminate a face. Even then, distance made it impossible for the men aboard to distinguish expression.

"No need of it, looks like," Steele went on, sensing the mass contempt directed towards him from two sides. "The word gets spread without it."

Sanchez grunted and shrugged, as resigned to what was happening as everyone else aboard.

At first, some of the hired guns had hurled curses towards the banks in response to the tacit revulsion aimed at them. Once, Ned McCall had come close to exploding a rifle shot at a farmer and his family. But Engle had stepped in front of the muzzle.

"Shit scared of us, I figure," Frank Potter called down from the wheelhouse deck to where Steele and Sanchez stood on the hurricane deck. "Hate our guts on account of the niggers. But ain't about to tangle with us after what we done to get this far."

The Virginian nodded absently in agreement with the man above him. Then continued to rake his narrow-eyed gaze over the people, the buildings and the open country, searching for the first hint of an attack.

But none came.

"Garrett reckoned to stop us at the start," he said softly, speaking aloud his thoughts. "The teamsters and the people at Tucker's Ferry were a bonus for him. He was counting on the *Mississippi Star* to finish us."

The grim-faced Mexican both nodded and grunted this time.

"But he'll know by now what happened to that tub and the men aboard her," Potter pointed out. "And I'm bettin' he won't just be sittin' on his butt cryin' tears."

As more and more miles of water were put behind the sternwheeler, the men aboard her became increasingly conscious of the truth of this. Indifferent now to the tacit hostility of the bystanders who stood out in the open to emphasize their hatred and contempt. Negroes and whites alike aboard the *Queen of the River* felt their nerves being stretched tighter and tighter.

Every natural feature of the landscape on either side which might offer cover to even a single rifleman was viewed with deep suspicion until it had been left far behind, beyond effective shooting range. Each time a bird squawked or a distant clap of thunder cracked, men whirled towards the sound, hands tightening on their guns. And sweat ran free and shiny over tense faces whenever Engle had to slow the sternwheeler and veer close to the bank to go around an obstacle.

No one was immune to these effects of expecting a sudden explosion of violence to end the lengthening period of serenity: but only Steele was angry at himself for experiencing them. For he knew and understood simple fear of overt danger—and had learned to use this to his advantage. But nervousness of the unknown—akin to a child's terror of the dark—was new to him and he recognised it as devoid of reason.

But, once infected by it, it was difficult to shake off. Perhaps impossible in the confinement of a small riverboat, living around the clock in intimate closeness with others suffering the same symptoms.

Then Felicity Engle died and the Virginian immediately came to terms with the kind of fear he knew of old. The hard, ice cold ball in the pit of his stomach. A core of concentrated emotion that quickened a man's reflexes and sharpened his wits. A weapon as effective as a gun or a knife for as long as a man could control it from breaking up and spreading—to his brain to cause panic and to his limbs to start them trembling.

Twin Creeks was a single street town, the street ending at a small landing stage on the south bank of the river. It was named for the two streams—now dried up beds—which ran parallel with the street behind the back lots of the buildings on the east side.

The depot and supply camp for the railroad was a quarter mile west of town. There was a large station building, four roundhouses, and a broad area of stockyards. Gleaming, unused rails had already been laid from the depot to the piered timber and concrete bridge which spanned the two hundred feet wide Red River. Other tracks spurred off the main to the roundhouses, and ran through the stockyards.

Upwards of thirty cattlecars were parked on side-tracks. And each roundhouse held a big locomotive.

Behind the newly constructed depot were high piles of track and ties, neatly aligned wagons and a corral of horses.

And, as the *Queen of the River* reduced speed and nosed slowly towards the large landing stage beside the bridge, the horses appeared to be the only living things within a hundred miles radius of Twin Creeks. For that was how far the people aboard the sternwheeler seemed to be able to see in the mid-morning light of the sun. Both Texas on one bank and Indian Territory on the other were flat and grassy, sparsely featured with clumps of low brush and small outcrops of red rock.

Except for Campbell who remained at his engines and Engle who was in the wheelhouse, everyone aboard the boat was out on the open decks. First they anxiously surveyed the town, constantly moving eyes searching for a sign of life along the two rows of timber buildings facing each other across the broad street. Few trusted the apparent desertion—the lack of smoke from chimneys, the shuttered windows and tightly closed doors. All the business premises had painted signs on their facades, but only one such sign was noted by the newcomers: GARRETT STAGE AND FREIGHT LINE.

The town was astern of the boat, which was running in towards the landing stage under momentum with the sternwheel idle, when a dog howled. A man cursed and the dog became silent.

"I don't like it," Frank Potter complained, as all attention was switched from the town to the depot.

He, Steele, the cheroot-smoking City Sam Goldsmith and Felicity Engle were at the forward rail of the hurricane deck. The others, whites and Negroes, were clustered on the port side of the main deck below.

132

"Guess your old lady's whorehouse seems really swell now," the youthful Goldsmith replied.

"Come to think of it, even the old lady does," Potter came back, and tried a laugh.

"Shut up!" Felicity snarled.

Steele spared her a glance as she surfaced from a morass of misery for the first time since Sanchez had been allowed to get away with hitting her. In all that while, she had only emerged from her cabin when the boat halted for Moran and some Negroes to go ashore and fell trees for fuel. Then she had taken walks along the bank, morose and silent. Perhaps trying to salve her new-found insecurity.

But she had failed for, as the *Queen of the River* nudged the landing stage and Moran and Sanchez leapt ashore to secure the bow and stern lines, she revealed she was more terrified than anyone else aboard.

More than twenty fire arrows whooshed from the station building towards the docked vessel. The men who fired them had little time to take precise aim at predetermined targets. Just sufficient to strike matches, touch the flames to oiled rags, throw open window shutters and doors, and release taut bowstrings.

By then, the men aboard who had chosen to walk the narrow line between life and death had adjusted from fear of the unknown to concern for recognizable danger.

And Felicity Engle was dying.

She alone was hit by an arrow, the metal tip sinking into her right shoulder. She grunted at the impact and staggered to the side, slamming into Potter as the man went down into an instinctive crouch. Then she screamed as she started to topple across the man, her shirt and hair bursting into flames.

Potter shrieked his own horror and straightened up

suddenly to lunge into a retreat. The woman was lifted high—and tipped over the rail.

Below, the main deck was emptying as most of the men raced for the cover of the boiler and starboard companionway.

The rush of air around the falling figure served to fan the flames. And the crash of her body against the deck sprayed remnants of burning fabric away from her. She was conscious but unable to move, paralysed by agony or terror. Crumpled up on her side, she was unable to beat at the fire raging in her hair or burning along the lengths of her legs. Just to scream, high and loud enough for the pitiful sound to be heard above the crackle of rifle fire.

One of the men shooting was Andy Clapham, stretched out prone in the cover of the steam capstan over which Will Breen had died.

"Clapham!" Steele yelled, between two closely spaced shots at the depot's main building. "Get Mrs. Engle!"

The younger of the bearded brothers glanced to the side and saw the woman on fire, her scorched body almost naked now as the final pieces of charred clothing dropped off her. But her long hair continued to flame.

Bullets struck the capstan and ricocheted.

"I'm workin' for cash, buddy!" Clapham snarled, pressing himself tight to the deck. "Not friggin' medals!"

Fighting to keep his anger balled up as tight as his fear, Steele whirled and raced across the deck. Bullets cracked past his head and body. Smoke from a dozen small fires started by the arrows stung his eyes. The acrid taint of countless expended bullets bit into the membranes of his throat. The noise of gunshots and flames, roaring engines and a thrashing paddlewheel, screams

134

of terror and obscene shrieks of rage beat against his eardrums.

He went down the stairway four treads at a time, hit the main deck hard and straightened his legs to power a forward lunge.

Felicity Engle was not on fire any more. She made no sound nor movement. With the Colt Hartford clutched in one hand, Steele used the other to grasp the elbow of an outstretched arm.

The sternline snapped and the *Queen of the River* swung suddenly away from the landing stage. Steele almost stumbled to the deck as he dragged the woman away from where she had fallen.

Men cursed and screamed as they fought each other to find new cover, their positions suddenly exposed as the boat came about, still linked to the shore by the bow line.

The Virginian dragged his inert burden to the pile of logs forward of the boiler.

Stan Clapham was there, one hand pressed tight to his eyes. His body was shaking. Two Negroes lay close to him, one with a bullet hole in his chest and the other with a pool of blood where his left eye had been. But the bearded white man was not crying for the dead blacks.

Steele looked up from the woman as the engines changed note, the paddles halting momentarily before restarting in reverse.

Andy Clapham had not been fast enough in compensating for the boat's turn. He had been hit by at least six bullets in the head and body. In either voluntary response or perhaps by the sheer velocity of impact, he had been sprawled out on his back on the open deck, showing to all who cared to look the many holes which continued to pump blood along his right side.

"Forget him and her for now, feller," the Virginian

said, and pointed to the charred corpse of Felicity Engle as the surviving Clapham brother dropped his hands to reveal his red-rimmed eyes. "It's on account of fellers like that we're here."

The bow line parted and the boat seemed to leap backwards through the water as Steele nodded towards the two dead Negroes.

"You figure we got a chance in a friggin' million, buddy?" Clapham croaked around the lump in his throat. "If you do, you aren't near so smart as I took you for."

Both men looked across the top of the logs as the area of water between the bow and the landing stage widened.

All gunfire from the station building had stopped. And there was little shooting from the *Queen of the River*. They could see the faces of the enemy at windows and doorways: some watching with icy calmness while others grinned their triumph.

Then a line of cattlecars began to move, rolling slowly down the gentle incline through the stockyards as a man in the brake van operated his wheel.

The riverboat came to a shuddering halt and, for a moment, a new sound was added to the lessening noise in the battle's lull: the splintering of wooden paddles as the sternwheel smashed itself to pieces on one of the bridge's concrete piers.

"I lost power!" Engle bellowed. "I couldn't steer her! Why wasn't no one on the friggin' boiler!"

Nobody replied and Engle, rushing from the wheelhouse, came to an abrupt halt, exposed and vulnerable on the open top deck. Held in the invisible grip of inevitable defeat, he survevyed the separate parts of the approaching end.

Under him, the *Queen of the River* was blazing fiercely along her portside superstructure, the fire billowing up far more black smoke than her now cooling twin stacks ever had done. Her engines were silenced and the supports and connecting rods of her smashed sternwheel held her fast to the bridge pier.

Immediately ahead on the Texas side of the river, Wyatt Moran was crumpled in bloody death on the landing stage. The mute Mexican leaned on his up-ended Winchester, blood oozing between the fingers of his right hand pressed to his left upper arm.

Engle was unable to see the rest of his dead and injured.

Beyond Moran and Sanchez, the line of cattlecars moved inexorably down the incline—gathering speed and then slowing as it rattled over the pre-set switches to close with the station building.

Downriver, Twin Creeks was no longer pretending to be deserted. People had emerged from the houses and business premises to form a long line along the rear of the buildings on the west side of the street. Men, women and children. One man held a big German shepherd on a leash and the dog was quiet, watching the smoke-draped scene at the bridge and depot in the same detached way as the people.

The group was reminiscent of those who had witnessed the passage of the sternwheeler through Louisiana and Arkansas and into Texas. Except that there was no hostility or hatred or contempt or resentment. These people, aware of the total truth, simply watched and waited, knowing they would be affected, whatever the outcome, but unwilling to take an active role in producing a result.

In the other direction, perhaps two miles to the west, a stage coach was racing along the riverside trail. The driver was in a standing crouch on the box as he lashed a whip over the backs of his straining team.

"Shoot!" Engle shrieked. "Kill the bastards! Come

on, you sonsofbitches! Do what I'm paying you for!"

The cause of his outburst was the sight of a score of men—carrying rifles and with their holsters tied down to their thighs—racing out of the station building and leaping aboard the rolling cattlecars. Men like the Claphams and Merv Conners, Will Breen, Ned McCall and Duke Fargo. Gunfighters who dressed for their trade and toted the utilitarian weapons of defense and attack.

"Why don't somebody tell the man," Stan Clapham muttered. "We been beat."

"You go tell him, feller," the Virginian replied.

The bearded man spat at a log six inches in front of his mouth. "You know why, buddy. In our line of business there's more than one Vic Krantz."

Only Cliff Engle ignored the threat of the many guns riding in the rolling cars as they ran across the bank at the end of the landing stage, the wheels setting up a sound of a different tone as they spun on rails fixed to the timber bridge. He continued to stand out on the open deck, frustrated by his own lack of a gun as he shrieked at his men to open fire.

The span of the bridge was level, but the momentum of the cars carried them out to a midway point so that they rolled to a halt immediately above the burning and helpless *Queen of the River*. Smoke from the blaze billowed and whirled, by turns obscuring and revealing the line of cars. When they could be seen, so could the gunmen in them, standing now, rifle stocks against their shoulders with barrels angled down at the sternwheeler.

At last Engle was silent, faced with the reality of being covered at the end by more guns than he had started with.

"Stan?" a man on the bridge yelled. "Ain't that Stan Clapham?"

"Yeah, George."

"Where's Andy?"

138

"You shot him."

"Dead?"

"As a man can get."

"Lousy shame, Stan. I still got his marker from that last poker game in Fort Worth."

"Morning, Jed!" Clint Burton called up to the bridge.

"You okay, Clint?"

"Little singed is all, Jed."

"Better than the Mexican. Caught one in the arm."

"Worse than Sanchez if I don't get off this boat soon," the Bostonian countered. "Either drowned or burned to a cinder."

"This is crazy!" Engle bellowed. "It's like a crazy frigging nightmare! Men are dead and dying! The ship's going to . . . Goddamnit, you're all acting like old home week!"

Many who had listened to the exchanges between old friends had been gripped by the strange dream-like state Engle had spoken of. Steele was one of them, and he shook free of it at the same time as Engle.

And he had glimpsed, through the ever-moving smoke, the packages of dynamite sticks lashed to the underside of the bridge.

Then smoke blanketed the sky, the bridge and the cars again.

Steele lunged away from the logs to crouch behind the port side of the boiler.

"What you plan?" Clapham asked, ducking down beside the Virginian.

"Figure she'll stay afloat awhile longer!" a new voice called down from the cattlecars. There was authority in his tone and it brought to an end the half humorous, half anxious shouting between boat and bridge. "Stage comin' and I figure Mr. Garrett's on it."

Steele whispered to Clapham against the bellowing

139

voice and pointed with one gloved hand towards the dynamite.

"We never did have no chance, did we?" Clapham rasped, pumping the action of his Winchester.

The Virginian saw that, back at the landing stage, the mute Mexican was watching him. Then Sanchez looked at the bridge—no longer leaning on his rifle, instead holding it around the frame low at his side, angled slightly upwards.

"And we could kill our stupid selves doin' this."

"If it had been easy, Engle wouldn't have needed us," the Virginian pointed out.

"The hell with that!" Engle roared in reply to the news of Garrett's arrival. "We're not waiting! I'm master of this ship!" He put more power into his voice. "Everybody aboard her. Over the side. Abandon ship!"

"Hey, where's Clapham and the guy was with him?"

For the first time, there was a note of fear in a voice calling from the bridge.

"It's a trick!" another man yelled, also afraid. "We gotta let 'em have it, Hogan!"

He fired without waiting for an order. And Burton died with a surprised expression on his face and blood torrenting from a gaping hole in the nape of his neck. There was just a gentle ooze of crimson from the wound in his throat.

Then three more rifle shots exploded. Steele and Clapham squeezed their triggers in unison. Sanchez was a fraction of a second late, having to help the Winchester up to his shoulder with his wounded arm.

Three bundles of dynamite were detonated at fifteen feet intervals along the bridge beneath the cattlecars. And tongues of yellow flame set off the rest.

Steele closed his eyes tight against the brilliant glare and dropped the rifle to hook his hands around a boiler pipe as the blast swept over and around him. He was deaf for stretched seconds, as he remembered a barren desert in the Great Basin when a lucky bullet had first proved to him what the newly invented blasting powder could do.

This time it was not army wagons which were destroyed and Shoshone Indians who died. Instead, a railroad bridge and a bunch of hired gunmen. Human flesh, timber and metal was ripped apart and hurled high in the morning air. A sheet of flame—red, yellow and blue—hung like a drape curtain for an instant, then was blasted into disappearing fragments. Balls of choking black smoke burst and then billowed, hiding the sun for longer than the flame.

Then the debris began to rain down. A piece of twisted rail. A still flaming chunk of wood. A dismembered arm, with part of a rifle stock still clutched in the fingers. Then half a head attached by bloody sinew to a portion of shoulder. More metal and timber. A whole body, naked, black and hairless as the corpse of Felicity Engle.

The *Queen of the River* was within the area of the ghastly torrent of death and destruction, but drifting clear. For the blast had torn her free of the pier, tilting her dangerously close to a capsize before she righted herself. The tilt had extinguished some of the flames and skittled men across her decks. But still she burned as, shocked and dazed and bleeding, whites and Negroes got to their feet and gazed at the carnage all around them.

More fires, started along her length by flaring timber from bridge and cattlecars, raged flames and billowed smoke.

Steele and Clapham came erect, the Virginian looking towards the Texas bank and the bearded man searching for his brother's body. But the corpse was gone. For anything not fixed fast to the sternwheeler had been flung across the decks and tipped into the river by the blast and the list.

Then Clapham grunted his satisfaction as he swung his gaze downriver. Several bodies were floating there, drifting on the calming water amid scattered pieces of blackened timber and unburned cordwood. Andy was recognizable. So were Felicity. And Clint Burton. A half dozen Negroes were also floating out there in the gentle current.

All this detritus of the violent explosion drifted gently towards the shore at the Twin Creeks landing stage. And the sternwheeler was on the same course, inching broadside on to where the townspeople continued to watch with inactive silence.

Men who did not trust the *Queen of the River* to ground against the bank before she was destroyed by the fires leapt overboard, those who could swim helping those who were driven into a fresh wave of panic by the water.

"So I was wrong," Stan Clapham said with a sigh. "We didn't get beat and we always had a chance."

Steele had already moved to the steam capstan in the bow where two men had died. Clapham spoke as he joined the Virginian. And others came running to form a group at the point where the burning riverboat would first touch the bank.

"We had the breaks," the Virginian replied, with a grimacing look towards the remains of the bridge. There were just truncated uprights jutting from the concrete piers, with twisted rails arcing down into the water from each bank. The ugly scene was bathed in bright sunlight again, for the smoke was now disintegrating before it reached the depot.

"Andy wouldn't see it that way," Clapham muttered.

"Nor that fancy talkin' Boston dude," Frank Potter added. "Mrs. Engle, neither."

"Felicity!" Cliff Engle wailed. Then got his voice and expression under control as all the men in the bow swung to look at him. Steele and Clapham. Potter and Goldsmith. Ned McCall and Campbell. A score of Negroes who had not chosen to abandon ship in mid-river. And Ricardo Sanchez on the shore, still bleeding badly from his wound after the exertion of moving along the bank from the depot to the town landing stage. "I'd forgotten."

"Best thing to do about the dead, feller," Steele responded. And received mental images of his father and Jim Bishop. "Hard to do, though," he added.

The corpses were already entangled in the pilings beneath the landing stage. And hidden from view as the boat sank her bow into the bank and swung around, to grind her burning port side against the dock.

The men leapt ashore, Engle claiming his right as master to be last off. He thudded his feet on the dry land just as the bow was wrenched clear, the currents reclaiming the sternwheeler to turn her out into mid-river again. She left her mark of fire burning the timbers of the landing stage as she started a slow spinning course down river.

Engle, Potter and Campbell watched her. Men who knew and had a feeling for riverboats. Experiencing sadness as they witnessed her death throes.

The rest of the group, swelling in numbers as Negroes waded ashore and clawed up the bank, looked towards the approaching stage coach. Just as the townspeople did.

The driver kept the six horse team at a sweat-lathered gallop crossing the depot tracks: then slowed the animals skillfully to bring the stage to a smooth halt, sideways onto the gatherings and midway between them.

Under the dust of travel the stage was brand new, with polished woodwork and shined brass trim. The

143

name of Garrett's transportation company was painted on the door in gold-leaf.

"Cole!" Engle gasped as the door swung wide and a wizen-faced, stoop-shouldered, grey-haired old man stepped out.

"Cliff," one of the richest men in Texas, perhaps the country, said curtly. He glanced from the slowly turning riverboat to the wrecked bridge. "Me and Alex got here too late, looks like."

Alexander Garrett matched Cole Meline only in wealth and age. He was also in his eighties. But he was tall and heavy enough to tilt the stage as he stepped from it. And he stood ramrod straight under a full head of black hair.

"Damn shame," the bigger man muttered, not bothering to survey the scenes of destruction again.

Steele sensed the rising anger of the men around him. But Meline's matter-of-fact voice kept it in check for a while.

"You managed to make Felicity stay in New Orleans then, Cliff? About time you tamed that girl into doing what she's told."

"He learned too late, feller," the Virginian drawled. Meline stiffened.

"She's dead, you rich sonofabitch!" Ned McCall hissed. "Like Will and Duke. And a lot of others I don't give a shit about. On account of you and this other rich bastard left it too late to call it quits!"

Meline ignored the enraged McCall. Instead he overlaid his grief with a fury of his own—directing it at his son-in-law.

But Garrett was not immune to McCall's bitterness. "Lange!" he snapped as the scar-faced man burst from between Potter and Goldsmith, Colt drawn, cocked and levelled.

The stage driver had been aware of the ugly mood of

the gunmen and Negroes as they responded to the callous attitude of Meline and Garrett. And had already eased his cocked Remington halfway out of the holster. Now it came clear, was turned and fired. The bullet dove deep into McCall's chest, left of center.

"Partners," McCall gasped as he sank to the ground. Whether it was a call to the dead Breen and Fargo or a curse for Meline and Garrett, nobody knew. All eyes swung towards the sound of a second shot, less loud, from a tiny Derringer in Meline's hand. Sending a bullet into the open mouth of Cliff Engle as he stared at the falling McCall.

"For getting my little girl killed," the grey-haired old man announced flatly. And blew the stink of exploded powder from the muzzle of the small gun before he replaced it in his jacket pocket.

"Seems to me it was you and Mr. Garrett got all these people killed, buddy," Stan Clapham corrected, without rancor.

Lange still had the Remington in his hand, butt resting on his thigh and barrel aimed over the heads of the men below him. But the fresh killings had taken the edge of the mass anger.

"Apart from my daughter, you were all being paid to do a job," Cole Meline pointed out. "It doesn't matter that in the end the job was unnecessary." He sharpened his tone. "Where the hell do you think you're going?"

The question was directed towards Steele, who had broken from the group and was moving to go around the stage towards the depot. He halted and held the Colt Hartford under his arm as he pulled off the buckskin gloves.

"Still owed a half day's pay, feller. Reckon I'll be happy to take it in kind. A horse from the corral. And some gear if there's any at the depot."

There was a muttering of approval and the other hired gunmen stepped forward to join the Virginian.

Only the blond and handsome Campbell remained with the Negroes, as pathetically lost and helpless as the blacks.

"You're all making a mistake," Garrett warned. "Now that me and Cole have patched up our differences and filed papers for a joint operation, this railroad will go through."

"And there'll be high-paying jobs for every man who wants one."

"Railroads ain't my line," Clapham answered.

"I'm a city boy," Goldsmith said.

"Missin' my old lady," Potter added.

Sanchez merely shook his head.

"I've been paid for working as much as I can take from you, feller," the Virginian drawled. He looked from the anxious Negroes to the shocked townspeople. "My part in this lousy mess is . . .

   . . . FINISHED."*

* * *

*Just this story. Adam Steele will be back again in the next book of the series.

Out of the American West rides a new hero.
He rides alone . . . trusting no one.

SPECIAL PREVIEW

Edge *is not like other western novels. In a tradition-bound genre long dominated by the heroic cowpoke, we now have the western anti-hero, an un-hero . . . a character seemingly devoid of any sympathetic virtues.* "A mean, sub-bitchin,' baad-ass!" *For readers who were introduced to the western via Fran Striker's Lone Ranger tales, and who have learned about the ways of the American West from the countless volumes penned by Max Brand and Zane Grey, the adventures of Edge will be quite shocking. Without question, these are the most violent and bloody stories ever written in this field. Only two things are certain about Edge: first, he is totally unpredictable, and has no pretense of ethics or honor . . . for him there is no Code of the West, no Rules of the Range. Secondly, since the first book of Edge's adventures was published by Pinnacle in July of 1972, the sales and reader reaction have continued to grow steadily. Edge is now a major part of the western genre, alongside ol' Max and Zane, and Louis L'Amour. But*

Edge *will never be confused with any of 'em, because Edge is an original, tough hombre who defies any attempt to be cleaned up, calmed-down or made honorable. And who is to say that* Edge *may not be a realistic portrayal of our early American West? Perhaps more authentic than we know.*

George G. Gilman created *Edge* in 1971. The idea grew out of an editorial meeting in a London pub. It was, obviously, a fortunate blending of concepts between writer and editor. Up to this point Mr. Gilman's career included stints as a newspaperman, short story writer, compiler of crossword puzzles, and a few not-too-successful mysteries and police novels. With the publication in England of his first *Edge* novel, *The Loner,* Mr. Gilman's writing career took off. British readers went crazy over them, likening them to the "spaghetti westerns" of Clint Eastwood. In October, 1971, an American editor visiting the offices of New English Library in London spotted the cover of the first book on a bulletin board and asked about it. He was told it was "A cheeky Britisher's incredibly gory attempt at developing a new western series." Within a few days Pinnacle's editor had bought the series for publication in the United States. "It was," he said, "the perfect answer to the staid old westerns, which are so dull, so predictable, and so all-alike."

The first reactions to *Edge* in New York were incredulous. "Too violent!" "It's too far from the western formula, fans won't accept it." "How the hell can a British writer write about *our* American West?" But Pinnacle's editors felt they had something hot, and that the reading public was ready for it. So they published the first two *Edge* books simultaneously; *The Loner* and *Ten Grand* were issued in July 1972.

But, just *who* is Edge? We'll try to explain. His name was Josiah Hedges, a rather nondescript, even innocent, monicker for the times. Actually we meet Josiah's younger brother, Jamie Hedges, first. It is 1865, in the state of Iowa, a peaceful farmstead. The Civil War is over and young Jamie is awaiting the return of his brother, who's been five years at war. Six hundred thousand others have died, but Josiah was coming home. All would be well again. Jamie could hardly contain his excitement. He wasn't yet nineteen.

The following is an edited version of the first few chapters, as we are introduced to Josiah Hedges:

* * *

Six riders appeared in the distance, it must be Josiah! But then Jamie saw something which clouded his face, caused him to reach down and press Patch's head against his leg, giving or seeking assurance.

"Hi there, boy, you must be Joe's little brother Jamie."

He was big and mean-looking and, even though he smiled as he spoke, his crooked and tobacco-browned teeth gave his face an evil cast. But Jamie was old enough to know not to trust first impressions: and the mention of his brother's name raised the flames of excitement again.

"You know Joe? I'm expecting him. Where is he?"

"Well, boy," he drawled, shuffling his feet. "Hell, when you got bad news to give, tell it quick is how I look at things. Joe won't be coming today. Not any day. He's dead, boy."

"We didn't only come to give you the news, boy," the sergeant said. "Hardly like to bring up another matter, but you're almost a man now. Probably are a man in everything except years—living out here alone in the wilderness like you do. It's money, boy.

"Joe died in debt, you see. He didn't play much poker, but when he did there was just no stopping him."

Liar, Jamie wanted to scream at them. *Filthy rotten liar.*

"Night before he died," the sergeant continued. "Joe owed me five hundred dollars. He wanted to play me double or nothing. I didn't want to, but your brother was sure a stubborn cuss when he wanted to be."

Joe never gambled. Ma and Pa taught us both good.

"So we played a hand and Joe was unlucky." His gaze continued to be locked on Jamie's, while his discolored teeth were shown in another parody of a smile. "I wasn't worried none about the debt, boy. See, Joe told me he'd been sending money home to you regular like."

"There ain't no money on the place and you're a lying sonofabitch. Joe never gambled. Every cent he earned went into a bank so we could do things with this place. Big things. I don't even believe Joe's dead. Get off our land."

Jamie was held erect against this oak, secured by a length of rope that bound him tightly at ankles, thighs, stomach, chest, and throat; except for his right arm left free of the bonds so that it could be raised out and the hand fastened, fingers splayed over the tree trunk by nails driven between them and bent over. But Jamie gritted his teeth and looked back at Forrest defiantly, trying desperately to conceal the twisted terror that reached his very nerve ends.

"You got your fingers and a thumb on that right hand, boy," Forrest said softly. "You also got another hand and we got lots of nails. I'll start with the thumb. I'm good. That's why they made me platoon sergeant. Your brother recommended me, boy. I don't miss. Where's the money?"

The enormous gun roared and Jamie could no longer feel anything in his right hand. But Forrest's aim was true and when the boy looked down it was just his thumb that lay in the dust, the shattered bone gleaming white against the scarlet blood pumping from the still warm flesh. Then the numbness went and white hot pain engulfed his entire arm as he screamed.

"You tell me where the money is hid, boy," Forrest said, having to raise his voice and make himself heard above the sounds of agony, but still empty of emotion.

The gun exploded into sound again and this time there was no moment of numbness as Jamie's forefinger fell to the ground.

"Don't hog it all yourself, Frank," Billy Seward shouted, drawing his revolver. "You weren't the only crack shot in the whole damn war."

"You stupid bastard," Forrest yelled as he spun around. "Don't kill him. . . ."

But the man with the whiskey bottle suddenly fired from the hip, the bullet whining past Forrest's shoulder to hit Jamie squarely between the eyes, the blood spurting from the fatal wound like red mud to mask the boy's death agony. The gasps of the other men told Forrest it was over and his Colt spoke again, the bullet smashing into the drunken man's groin. He went down hard into a sitting position, dropping his gun, splaying his legs, his hands clenching at his lower abdomen.

"Help me, Frank, my guts are running out. I didn't mean to kill him."

"But you did," Forrest said, spat full into his face and brought up his foot to kick the injured man savagely on the jaw, sending him sprawling on to his back. He looked around at the others as, their faces depicting fear, they holstered their guns. "Burn the place to the ground," he ordered with low-key fury. "If we can't get the money, Captain damn Josiah C. Hedges ain't gonna find it, either."

Joe caught his first sight of the farm and was sure it was a trick of his imagination that painted the picture hanging before his eyes. But then the gentle breeze that had been coming from the south suddenly veered and he caught the acrid stench of smoke in his nostrils, confirming that the black smudges rising lazily upwards from the wide area of darkened country ahead was actual evidence of a fire.

As he galloped toward what was now the charred remains of the Hedges farmstead, Joe looked down at the rail, recognizing in the thick dust of a long hot summer signs of the recent passage of many horses—horses with shod hoofs. As he thundered up the final length of the trail, Joe saw only two areas of movement, one around the big oak and another some yards distant, toward the smouldering ruins of the house, and as he reined his horse at the gateway he slid the twelve shot Henry repeater from its boot and leapt to the ground, firing from hip level. Only one of the evil buzz that had been tearing ferociously at dead human flesh escaped, lumbering with incensed screeches into the acrid air.

For perhaps a minute Joe stood unmoving, looking at Jamie bound to the tree. He knew it was his brother, even though his face was unrecognizable where the scavengers had ripped the flesh to the bone. He saw the right hand picked almost completely clean of flesh, as a three fingered skeleton of what it had been, still securely nailed to the tree. He took hold of Jamie's shirt front and ripped it, pressed his lips against the cold, waxy flesh of his brother's chest, letting his grief escape, not moving until his throat was pained by dry sobs and his tears were exhausted. . . .

"Jamie, our ma and pa taught us a lot out of the Good Book, but it's a long time since I felt the need to know about such things. I guess you'd know better than me what to say at a time like this. Rest easy, brother, I'll settle your score. Whoever they are and wherever they run, I'll find them and I'll kill them. I've learned some special ways of killing people and I'll avenge you good." Now Joe looked up at the sky, a bright sheet of azure cleared of smoke. "Take care of my kid brother, Lord," he said softly, and put on his hat with a gesture of finality, marking the end of his moments of graveside reverence. Then he went to the pile of blackened timber, which was the corner of what had been Jamie's bedroom. Joe used the edge of the spade to prise up the scorched floor boards. Beneath was a tin box containing every cent of the two thousand dollars Joe had sent home from the war, stacked neatly in piles of one, five, and ten dollar bills.

Only now, more than two hours since he had returned to the farmstead, did Joe cross to look at the second dead man.

The scavenging birds had again made their feast at the man-made source of blood. The dead man lay on his back, arms and legs splayed. Above the waist and below the thighs he was unmarked, the birds content to tear away his genitals and rip a gaping hole in his stomach, their talons and bills delving inside to drag out the intestines, the uneaten portions of which now trailed in the dust. . . .

Then Joe looked at the face of the dead man and his cold eyes narrowed. The man was Bob Rhett, he recalled. He had fought a drunken coward's war, his many failings covered by his platoon sergeant Frank Forrest. So they were the five men who must die . . . Frank Forrest, Billy Seward, John Scott, Hal Douglas, and Roger Bell. They were inseparable throughout the war.

Joe walked to his horse and mounted. He had not gone fifty yards before he saw a buzzard swoop down and tug at something that suddenly came free. Then it rose into the air with an ungainly flapping of wings, to find a safer place to enjoy its prize. As it wheeled away, Joe saw that swinging from its bill were the entrails of Bob Rhett.

Joe grinned for the first time that day, an expression of cold slit eyes and bared teeth that utterly lacked humor. "You never did have any guts, Rhett," he said aloud.

* * *

From this day of horror Josiah Hedges forged a new career as a killer. A killer of the worst kind, born of violence, driven by revenge. As you'll note in the preceding material, Edge often shows his grim sense of irony, a graveyard humor. Edge is not like anyone you've met in fact or fiction. He is without doubt the most cold-bloodedly violent character to ever roam the West. You'll hate him, you'll cringe at what he does, you'll wince at the explicit description of all that transpires . . . and you'll come back for more.